Mighty Mighty **MONSTERS**

THE ABOMINABLE
Snow Kid

Raintree is an imprint of Capstone Global Library Limited, a
company incorporated in England and Wales having its registered
offi ce at 7 Pilgrim Street, London, EC4V 6LB – Registered company
number: 6695582

www.raintree.co.uk
myorders@raintree.co.uk

Text © Capstone Global Library Limited 2015

The moral rights of the proprietor have been asserted.

Printed and bound in China

ISBN 978 1 4062 7989 4
18 17 16 15 14
10 9 8 7 6 5 4 3 2 1

British Library Cataloguing in Publication Data
A full catalogue record for this book is available from the British
Library.

Mighty Mighty MONSTERS

THE ABOMINABLE Snow Kid

created by
Sean O'Reilly

illustrated by
Arcana Studio

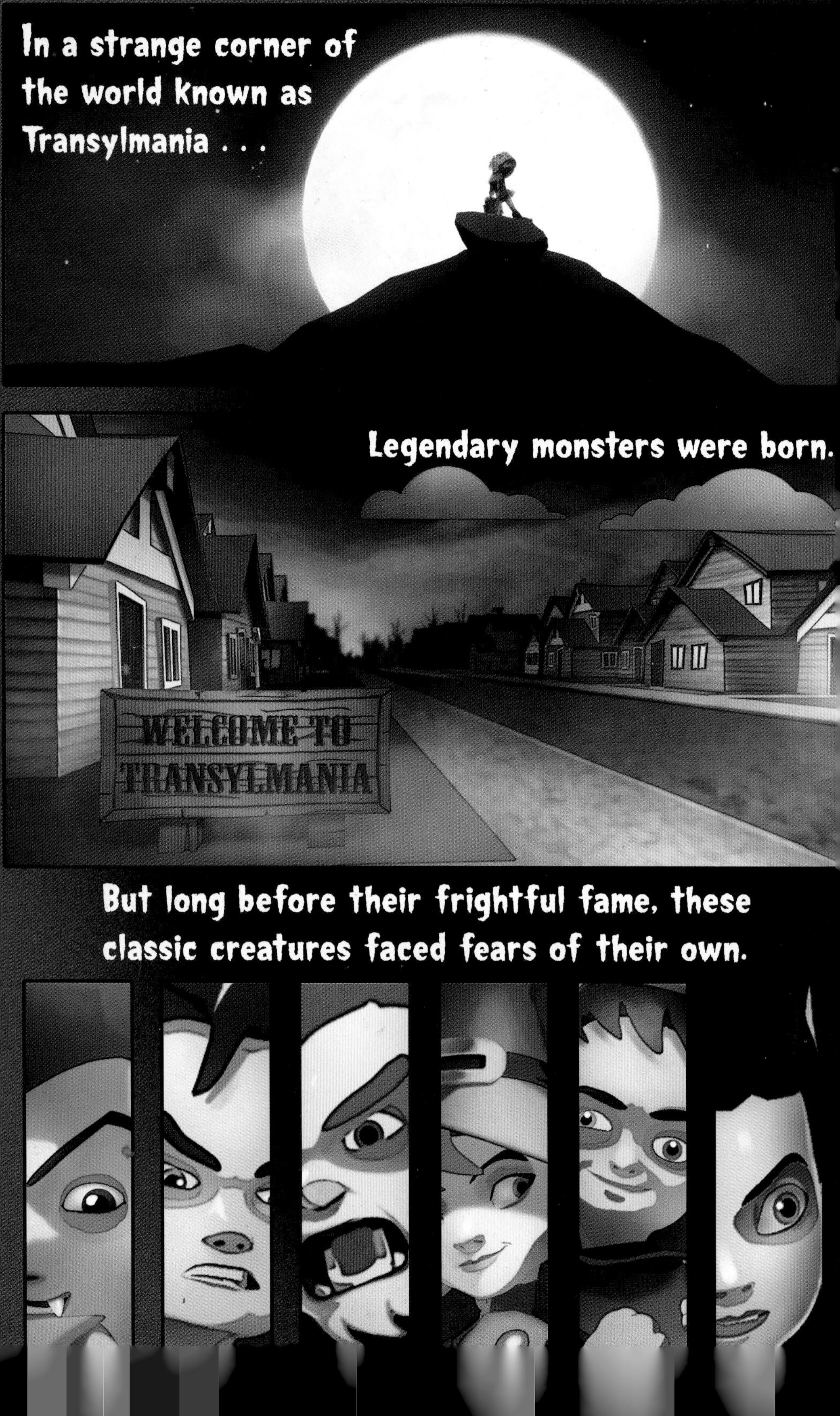
In a strange corner of the world known as Transylmania . . .
Legendary monsters were born.
WELCOME TO TRANSYLMANIA
But long before their frightful fame, these classic creatures faced fears of their own.

To take on terrifying teachers and homework horrors, they formed the most fearsome friendship on Earth . . .

Mighty Mighty MONSTERS

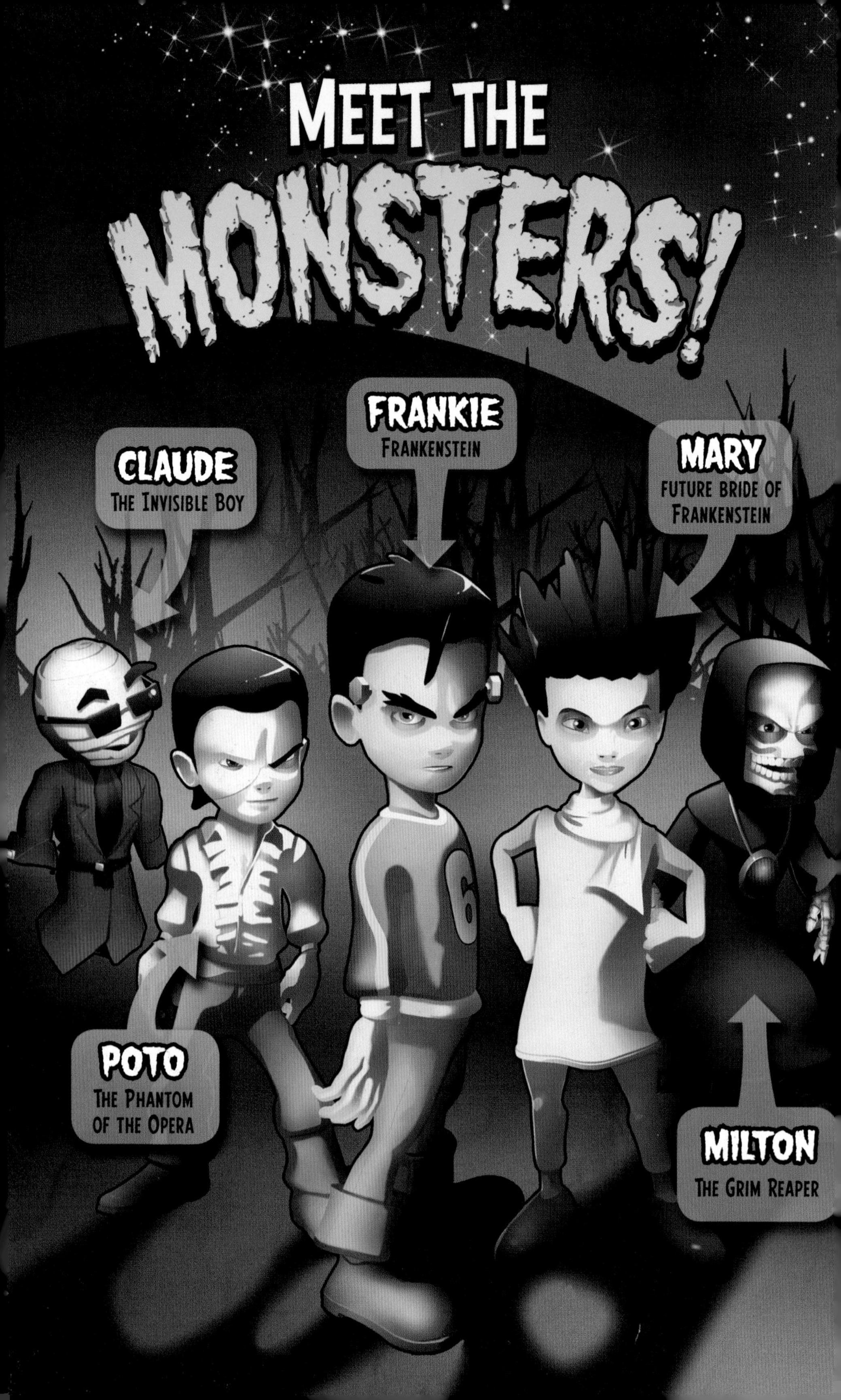
MEET THE
MONSTERS!
FRANKIE
FRANKENSTEIN
CLAUDE
THE INVISIBLE BOY
MARY
FUTURE BRIDE OF FRANKENSTEIN
POTO
THE PHANTOM OF THE OPERA
MILTON
THE GRIM REAPER

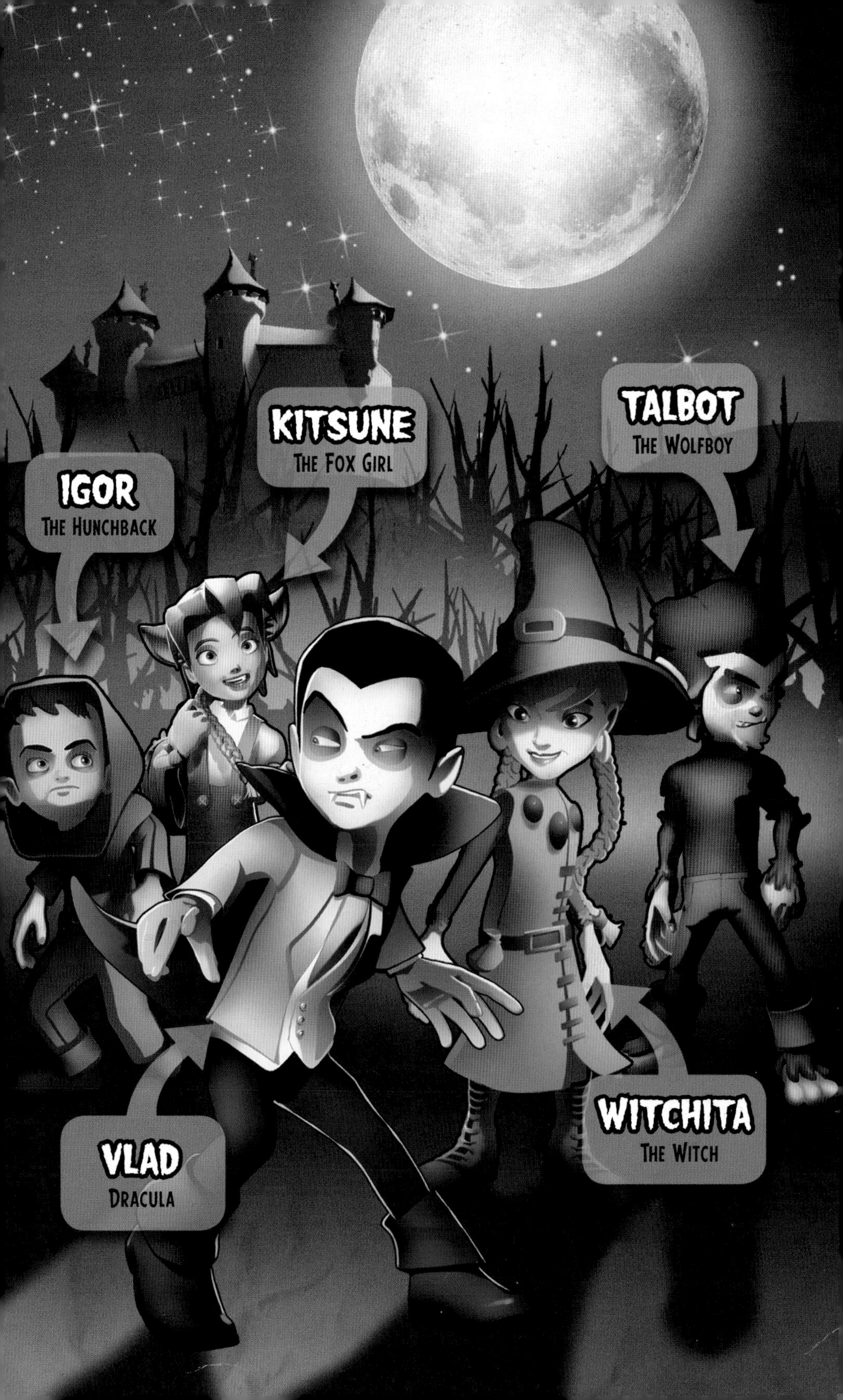
KITSUNE
THE FOX GIRL
TALBOT
THE WOLFBOY
IGOR
THE HUNCHBACK
VLAD
DRACULA
WITCHITA
THE WITCH

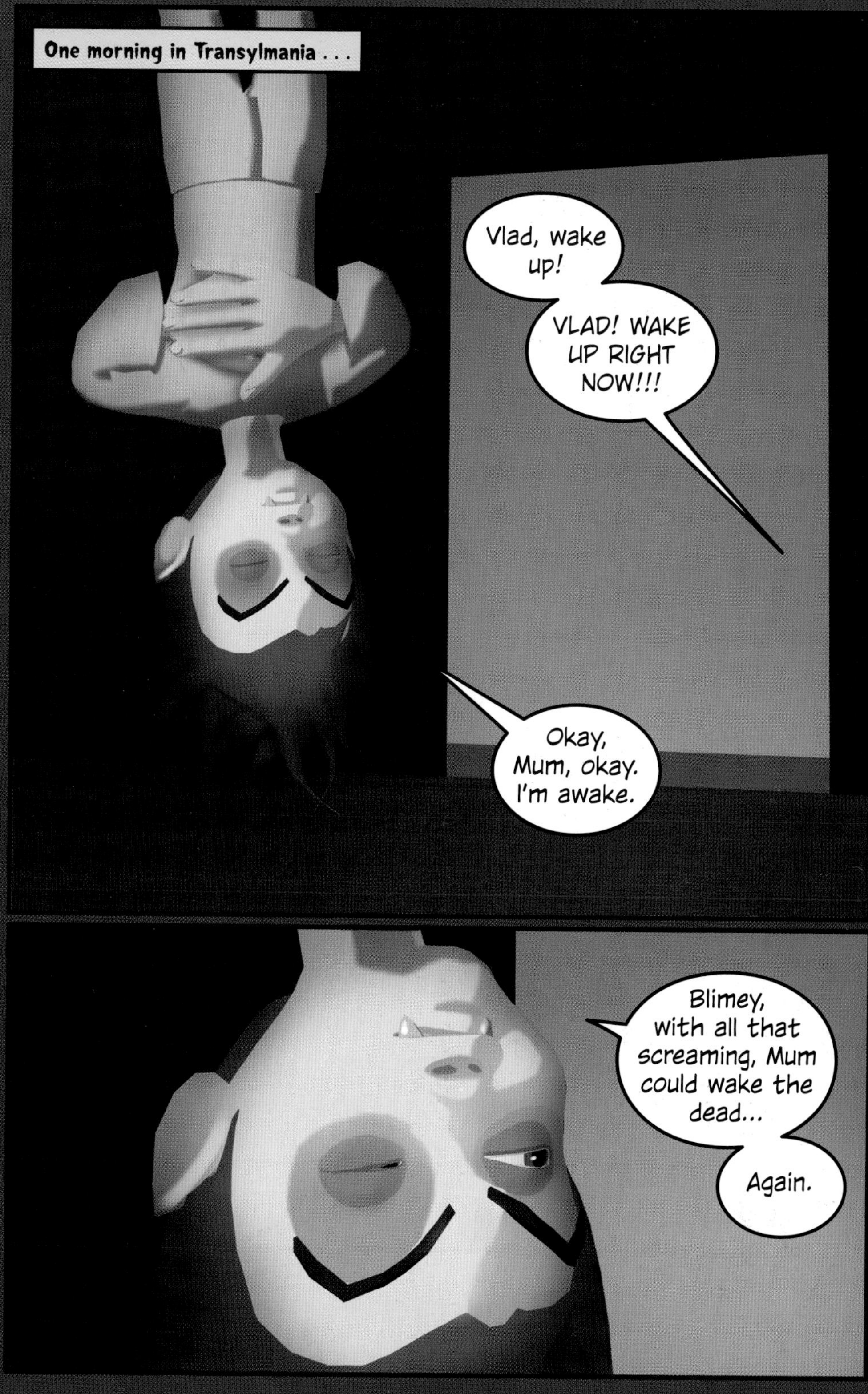
One morning in Transylmania . . .
Vlad, wake up!
VLAD! WAKE UP RIGHT NOW!!!
Okay, Mum, okay. I'm awake.
Blimey, with all that screaming, Mum could wake the dead...
Again.

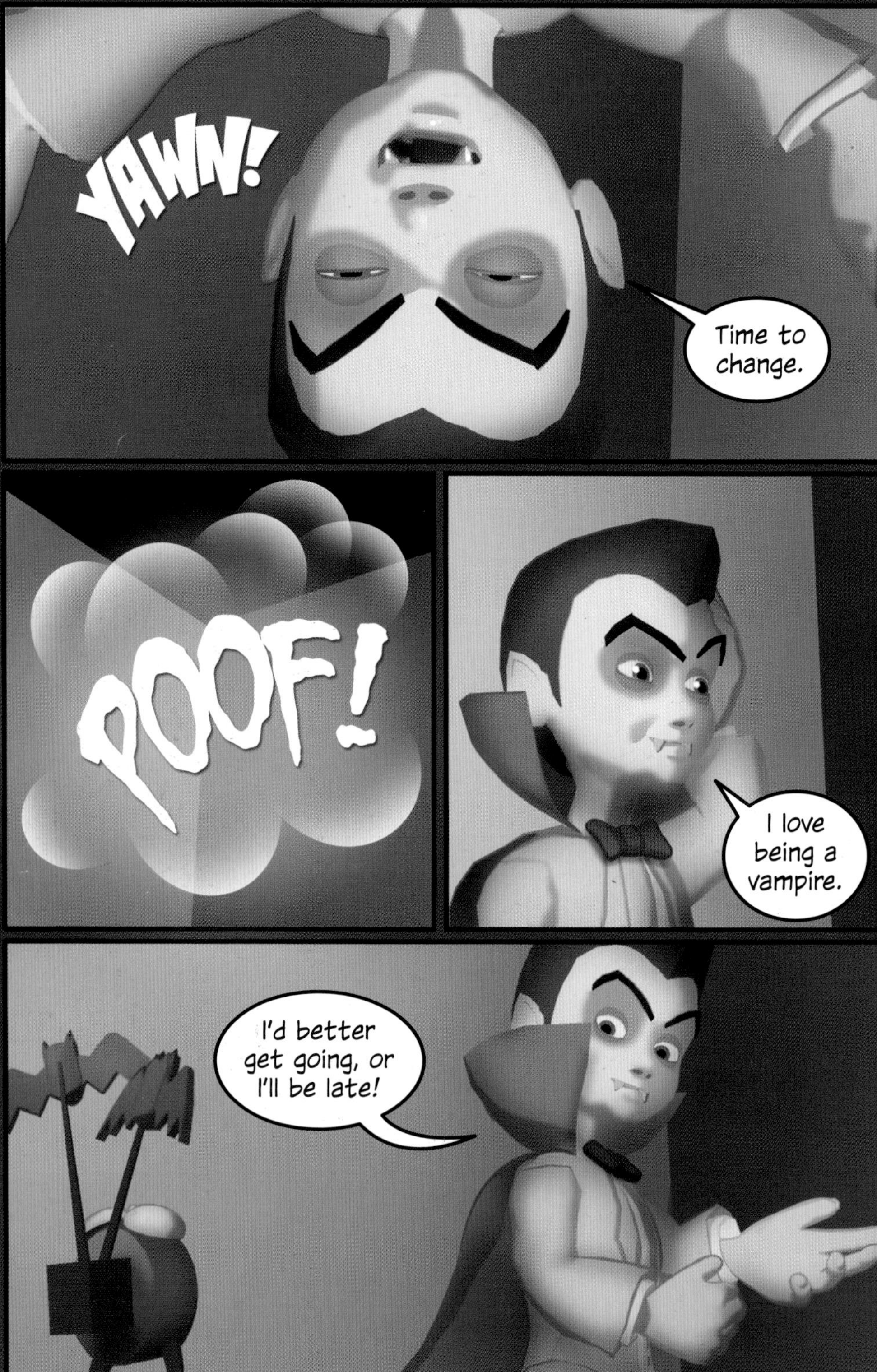
YAWN!
Time to change.
POOF!
I love being a vampire.
I'd better get going, or I'll be late!

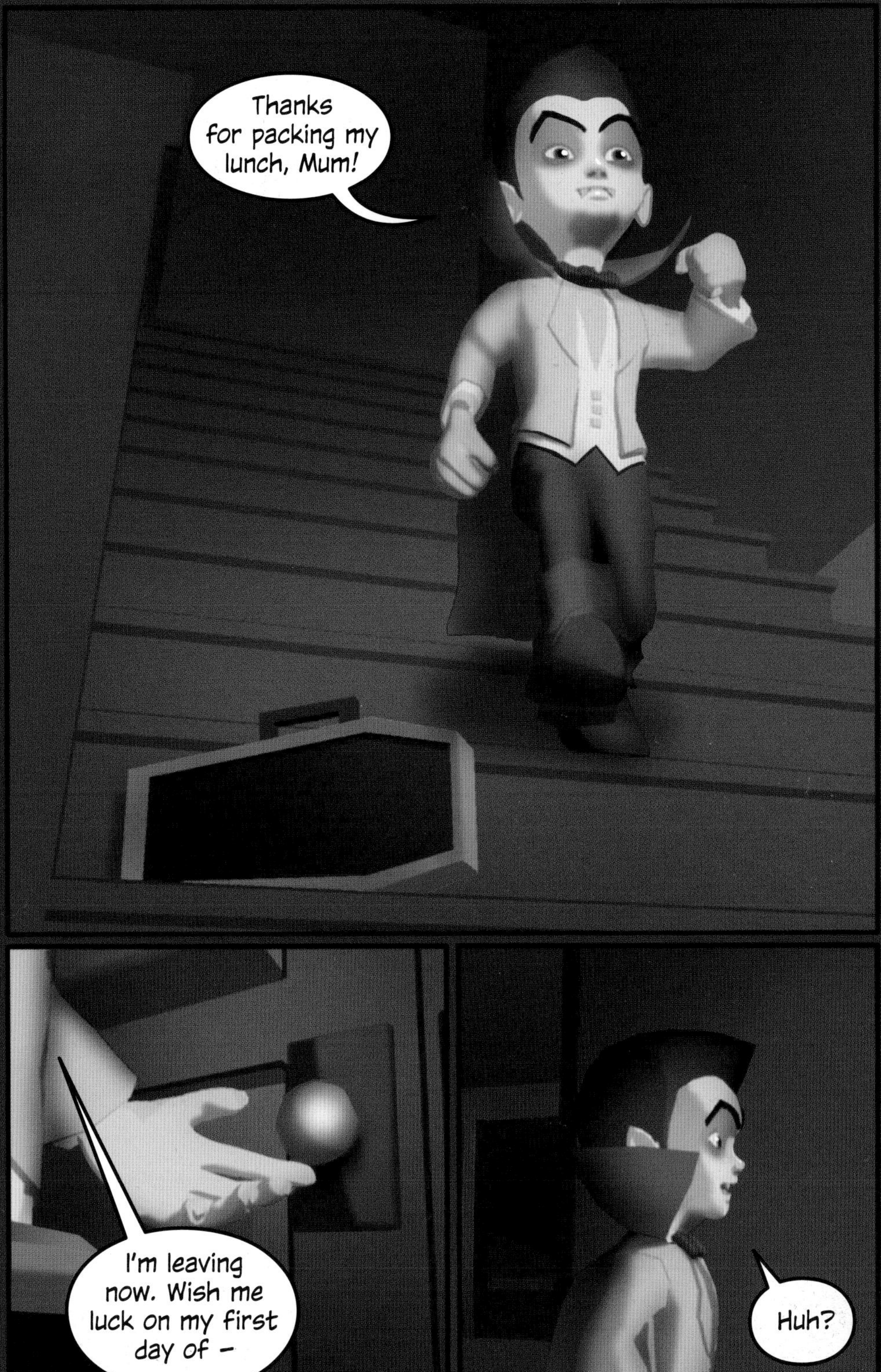
Thanks for packing my lunch, Mum!
I'm leaving now. Wish me luck on my first day of –
Huh?

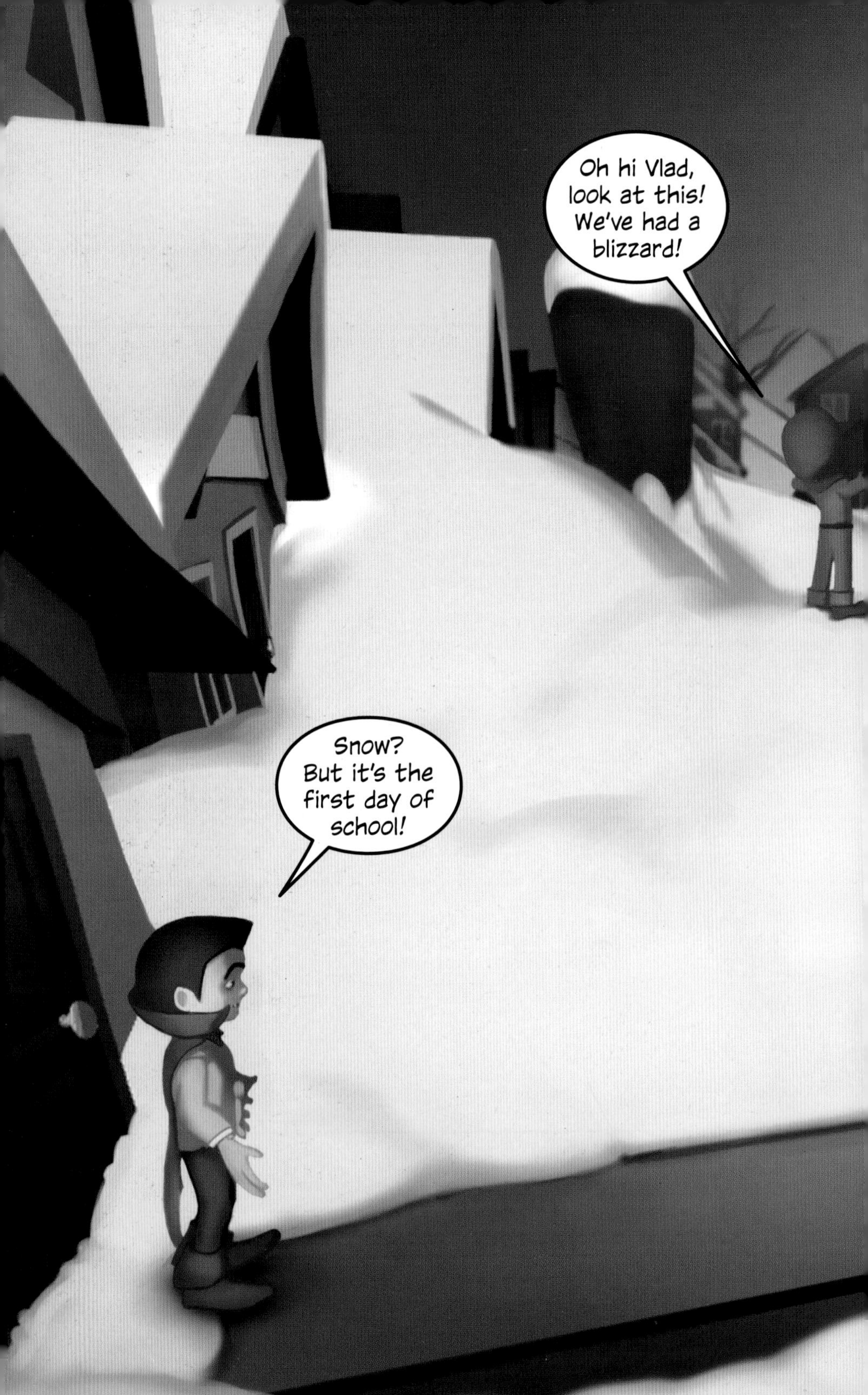
Oh hi Vlad, look at this! We've had a blizzard!
Snow? But it's the first day of school!

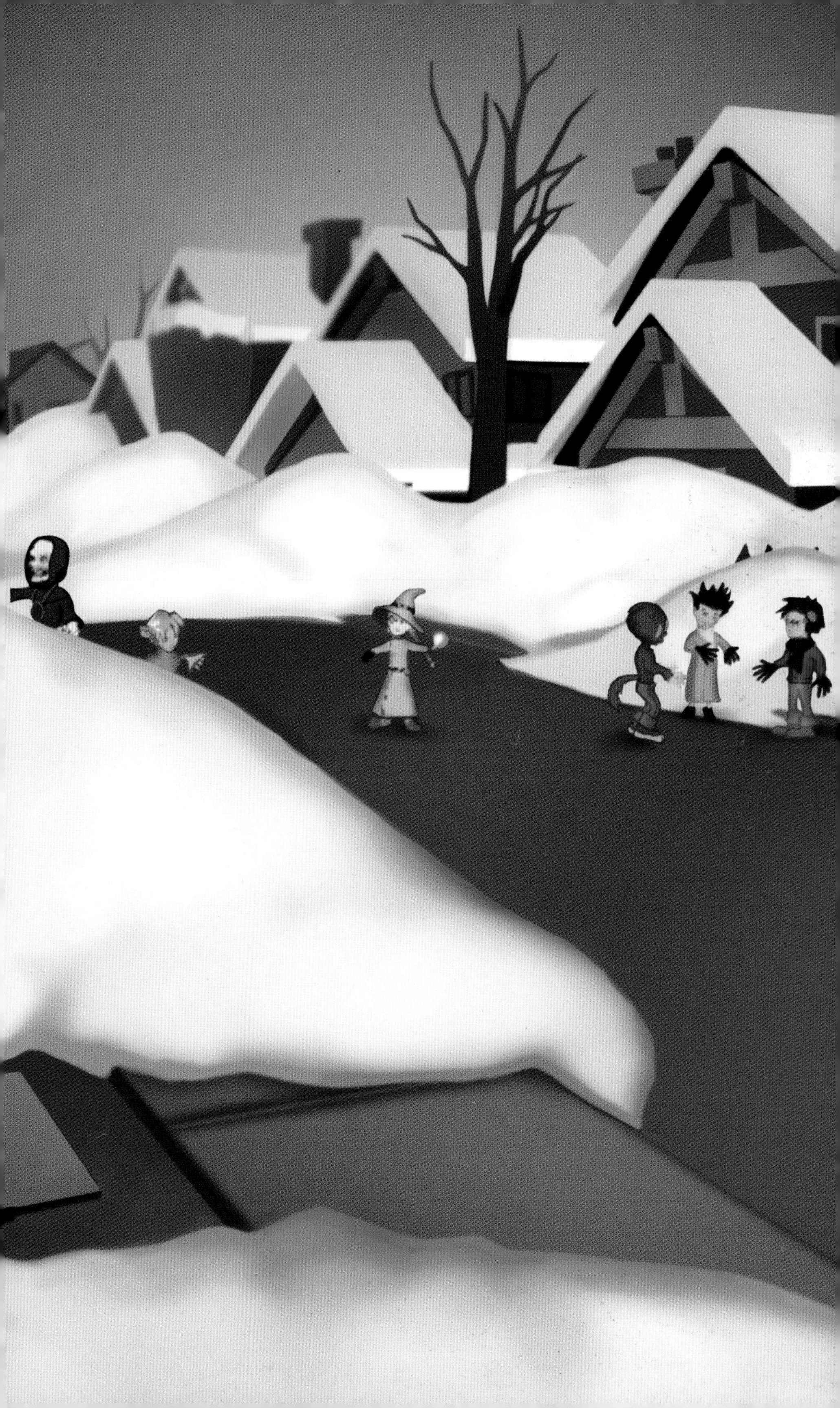

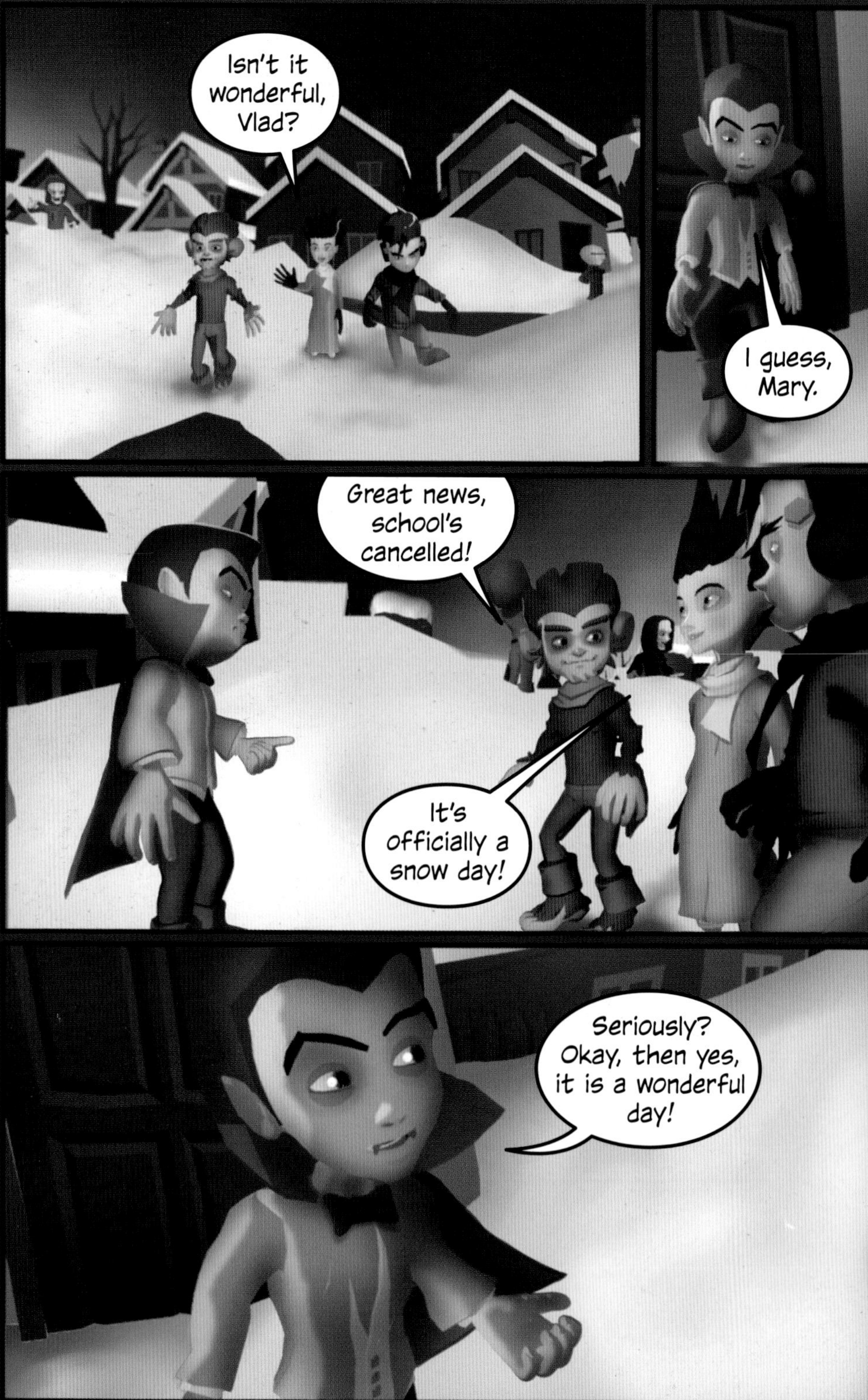
Isn't it wonderful, Vlad?
I guess, Mary.
Great news, school's cancelled!
It's officially a snow day!
Seriously? Okay, then yes, it is a wonderful day!

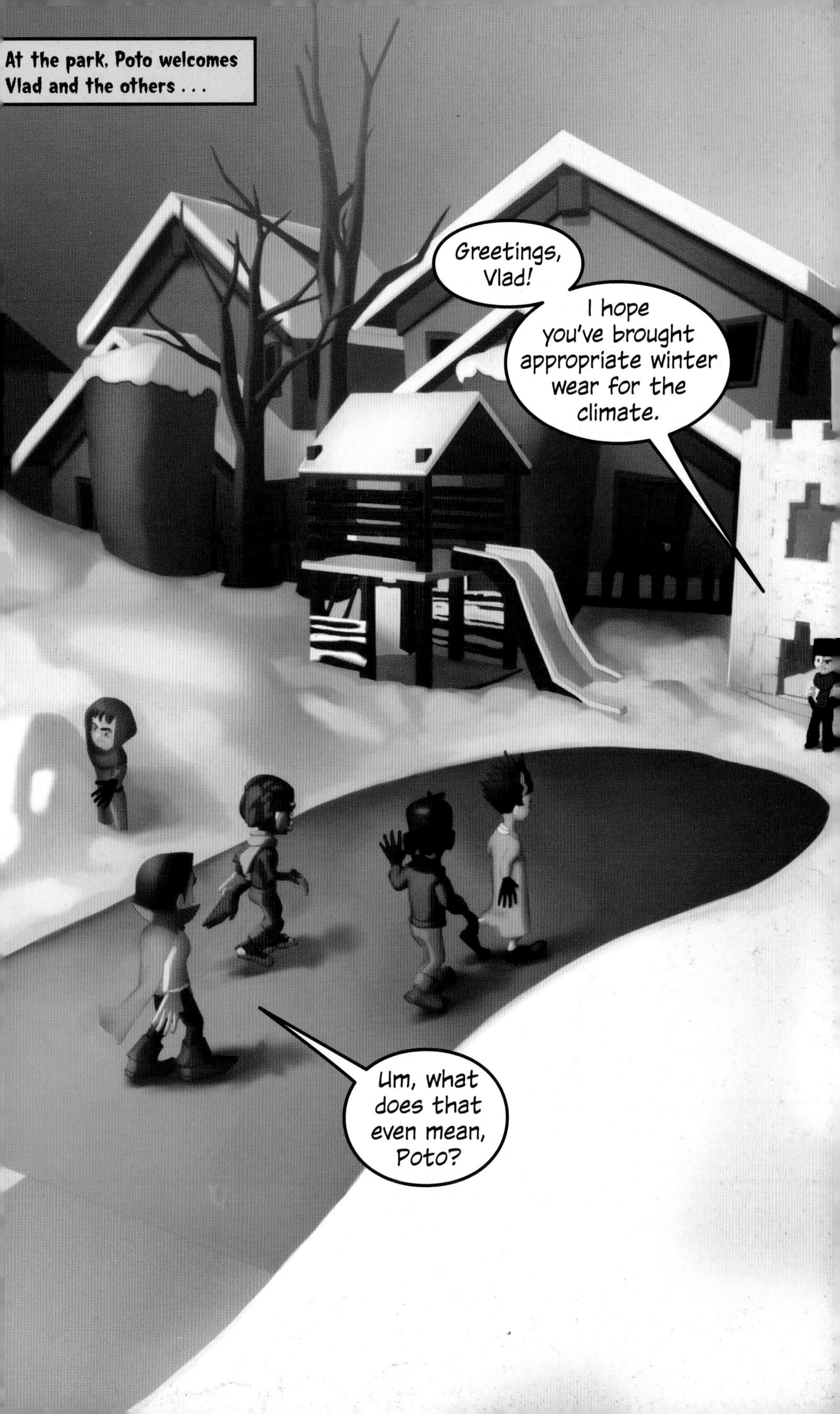
At the park, Poto welcomes Vlad and the others . . .
Greetings, Vlad!
I hope you've brought appropriate winter wear for the climate.
Um, what does that even mean, Poto?

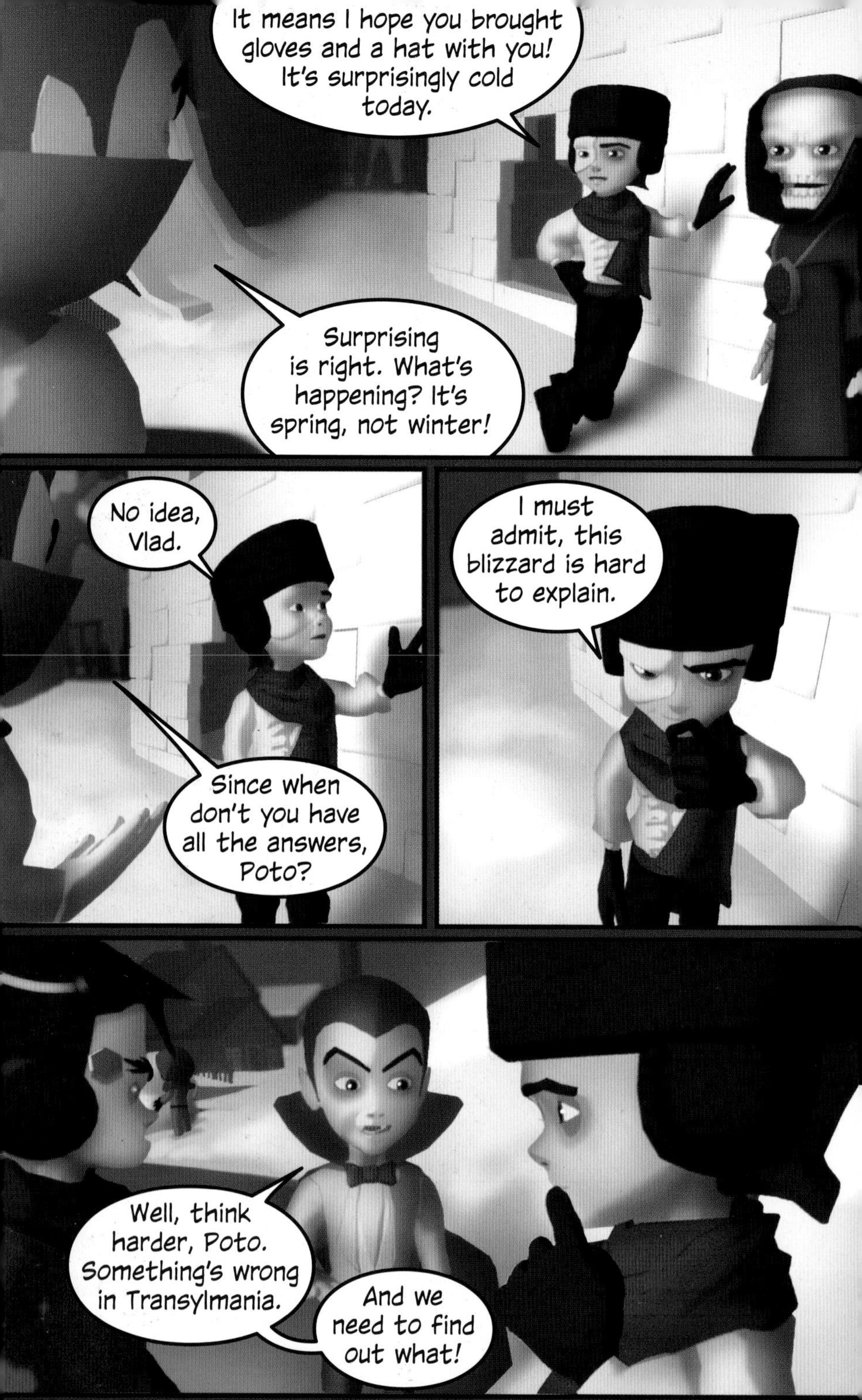

It means I hope you brought gloves and a hat with you! It's surprisingly cold today.
Surprising is right. What's happening? It's spring, not winter!
No idea, Vlad.
Since when don't you have all the answers, Poto?
I must admit, this blizzard is hard to explain.
Well, think harder, Poto. Something's wrong in Transylmania.
And we need to find out what!

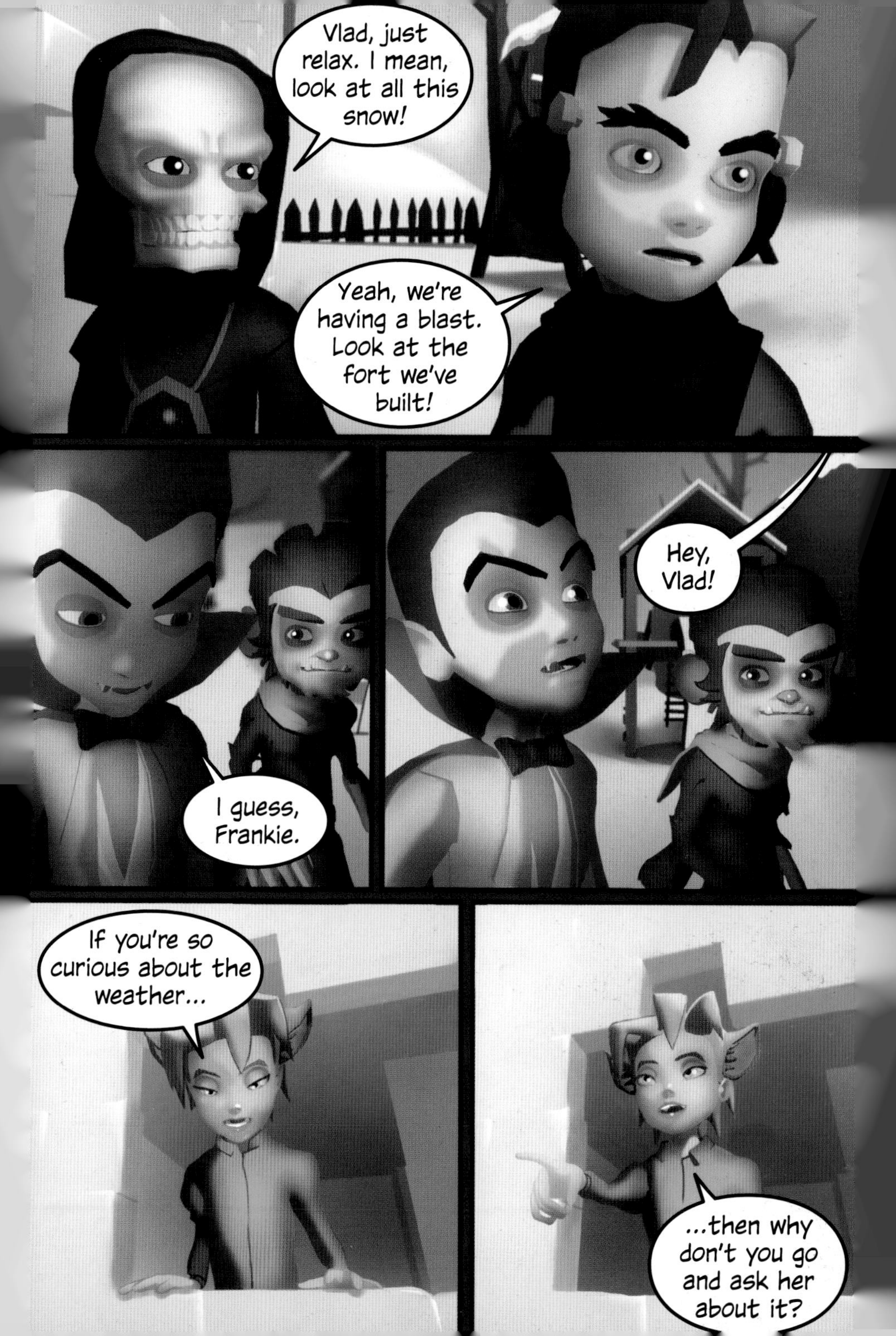
Vlad, just relax. I mean, look at all this snow!
Yeah, we're having a blast. Look at the fort we've built!
I guess, Frankie.
Hey, Vlad!
If you're so curious about the weather...
...then why don't you go and ask her about it?

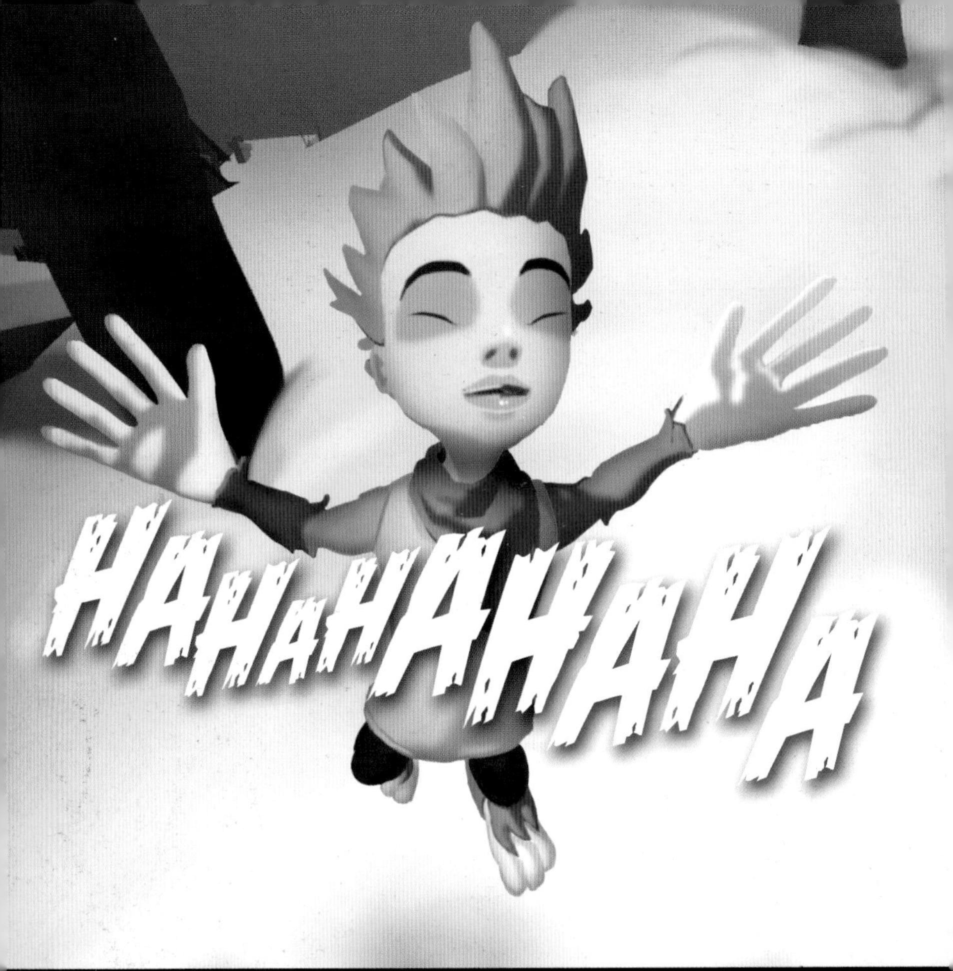
HAHAHAHAHAHAHA

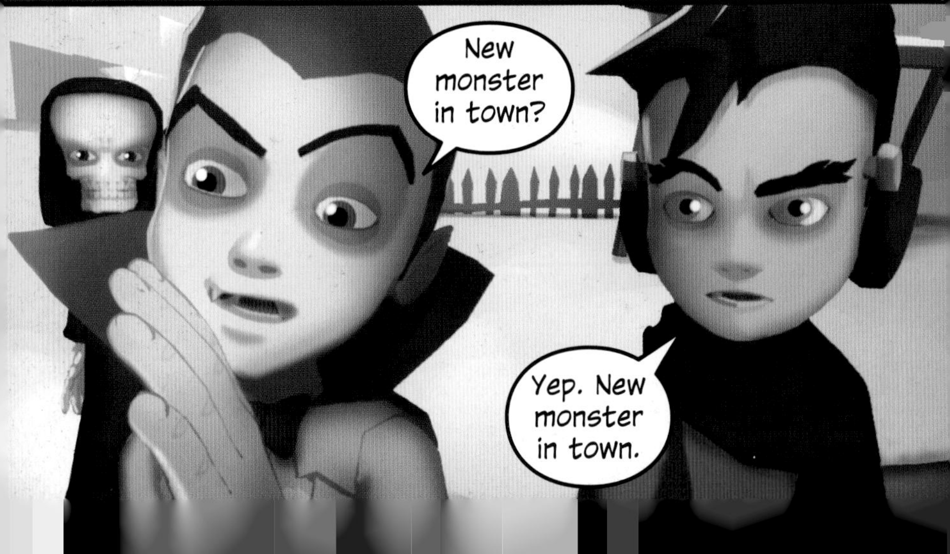
New monster in town?
Yep. New monster in town.

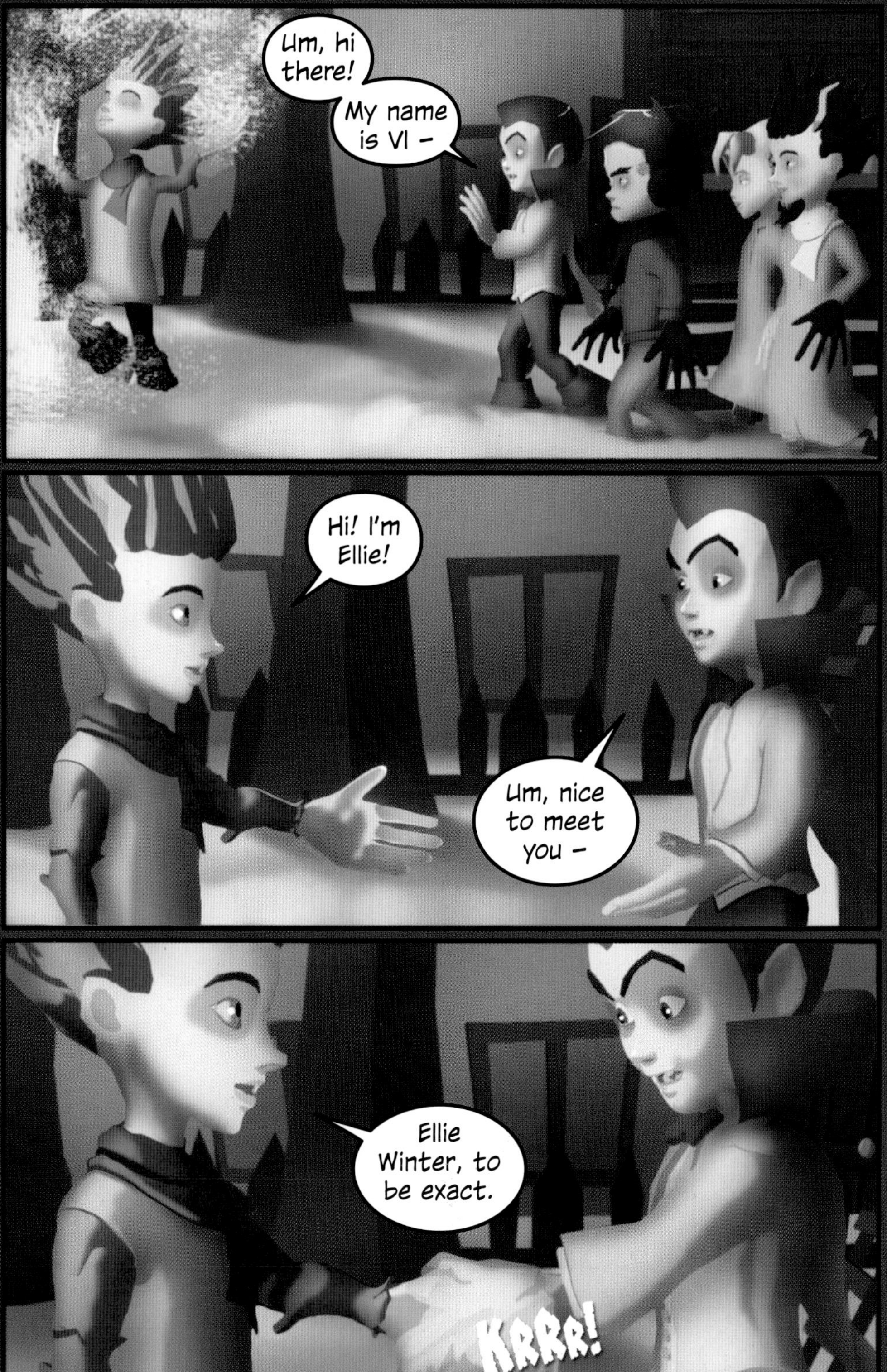
Um, hi there!
My name is Vl –
Hi! I'm Ellie!
Um, nice to meet you –
Ellie Winter, to be exact.
KRRR!

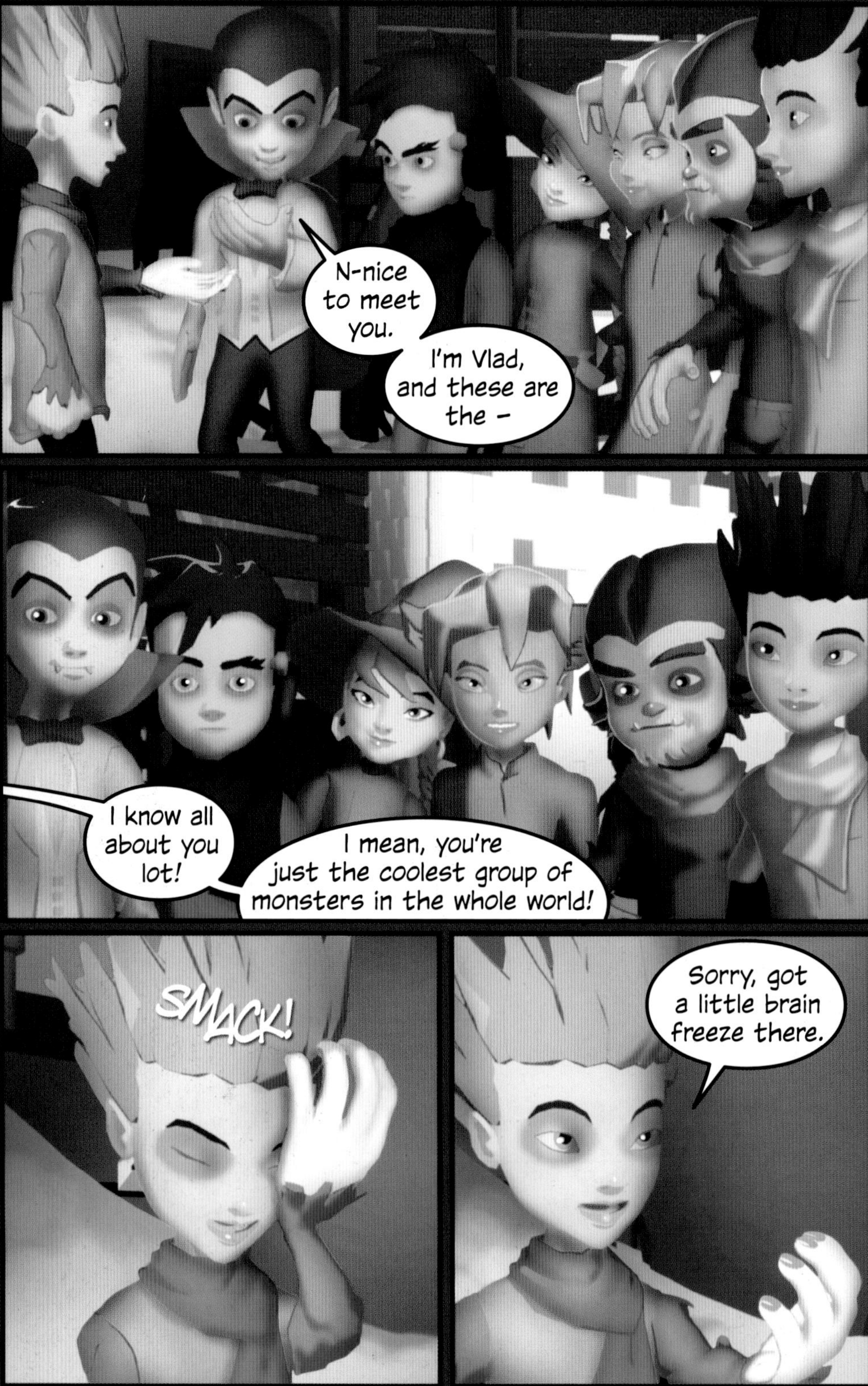
N-nice to meet you.
I'm Vlad, and these are the –
I know all about you lot!
I mean, you're just the coolest group of monsters in the whole world!
SMACK!
Sorry, got a little brain freeze there.

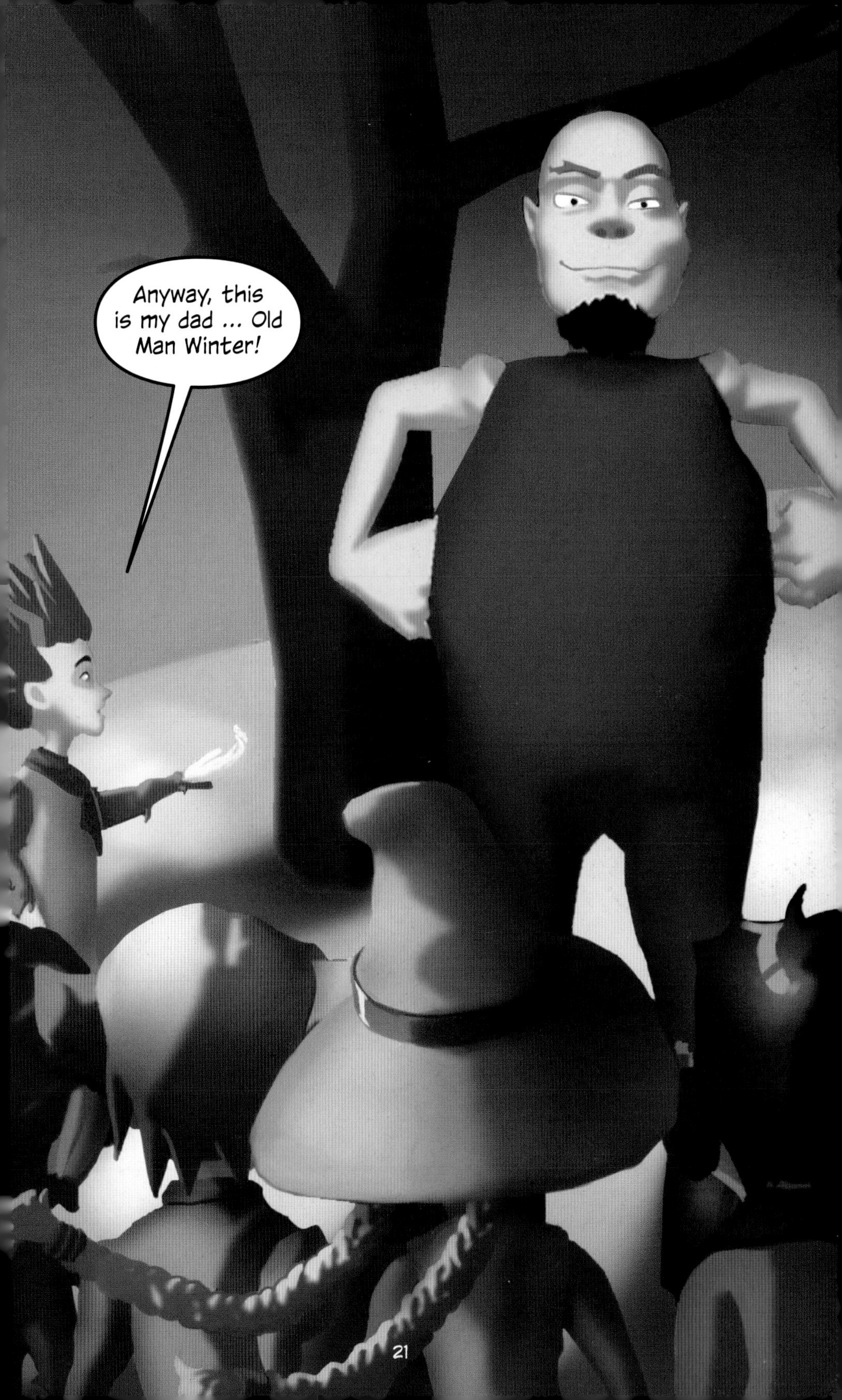
Anyway, this is my dad ... Old Man Winter!

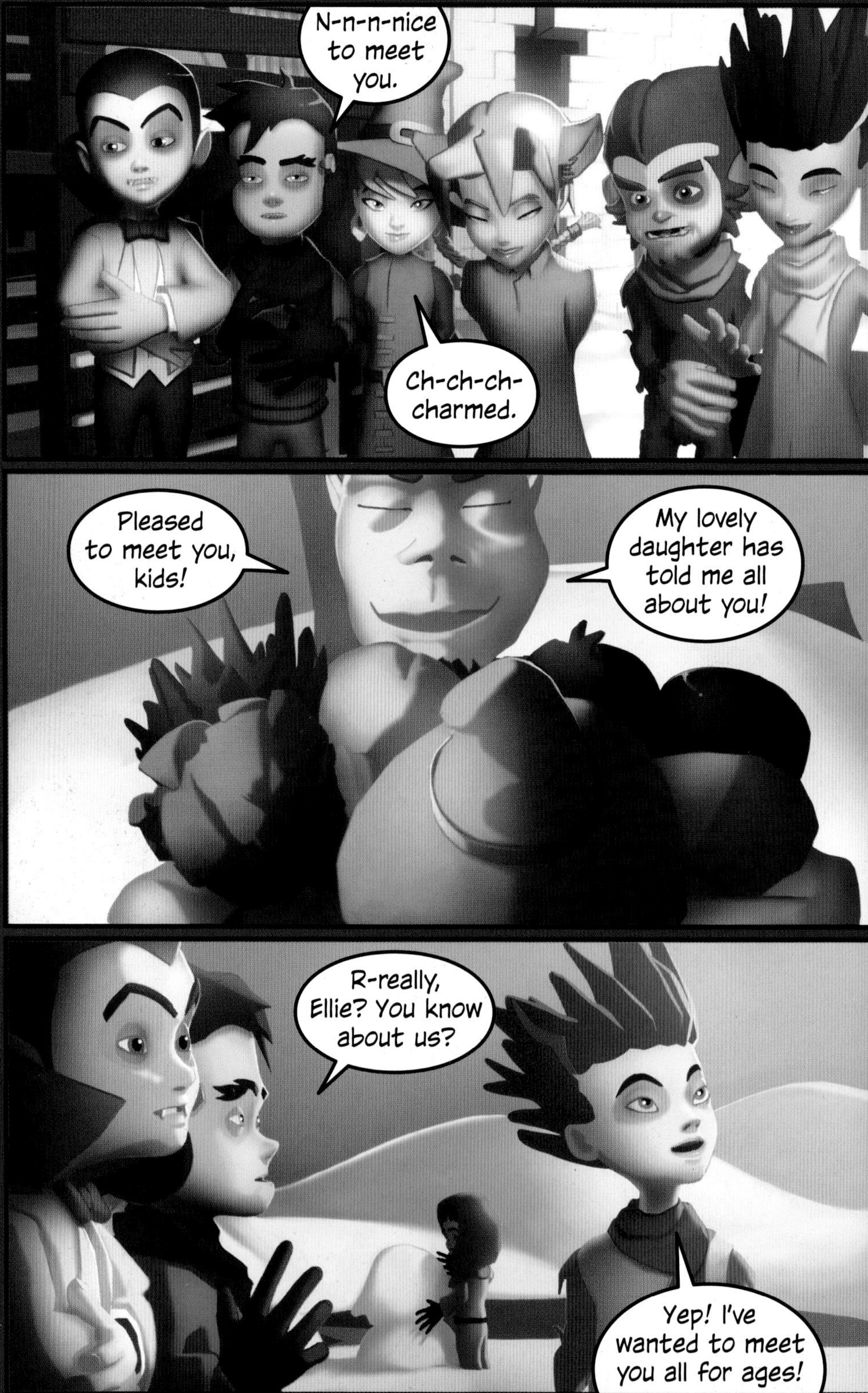
N-n-n-nice to meet you.
Ch-ch-ch-charmed.
Pleased to meet you, kids!
My lovely daughter has told me all about you!
R-really, Ellie? You know about us?
Yep! I've wanted to meet you all for ages!

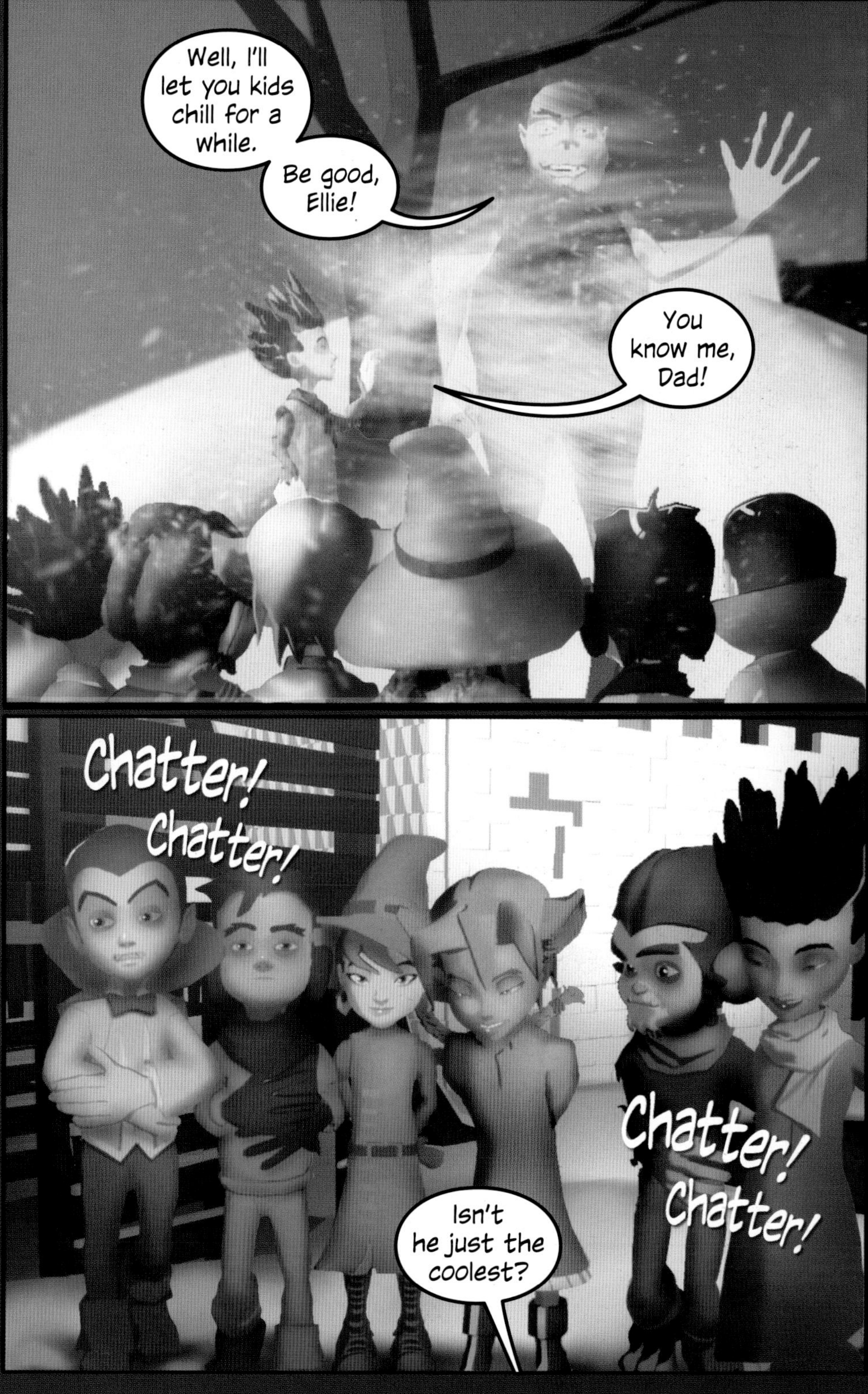
Well, I'll let you kids chill for a while.
Be good, Ellie!
You know me, Dad!
Chatter! Chatter!
Chatter! Chatter!
Isn't he just the coolest?

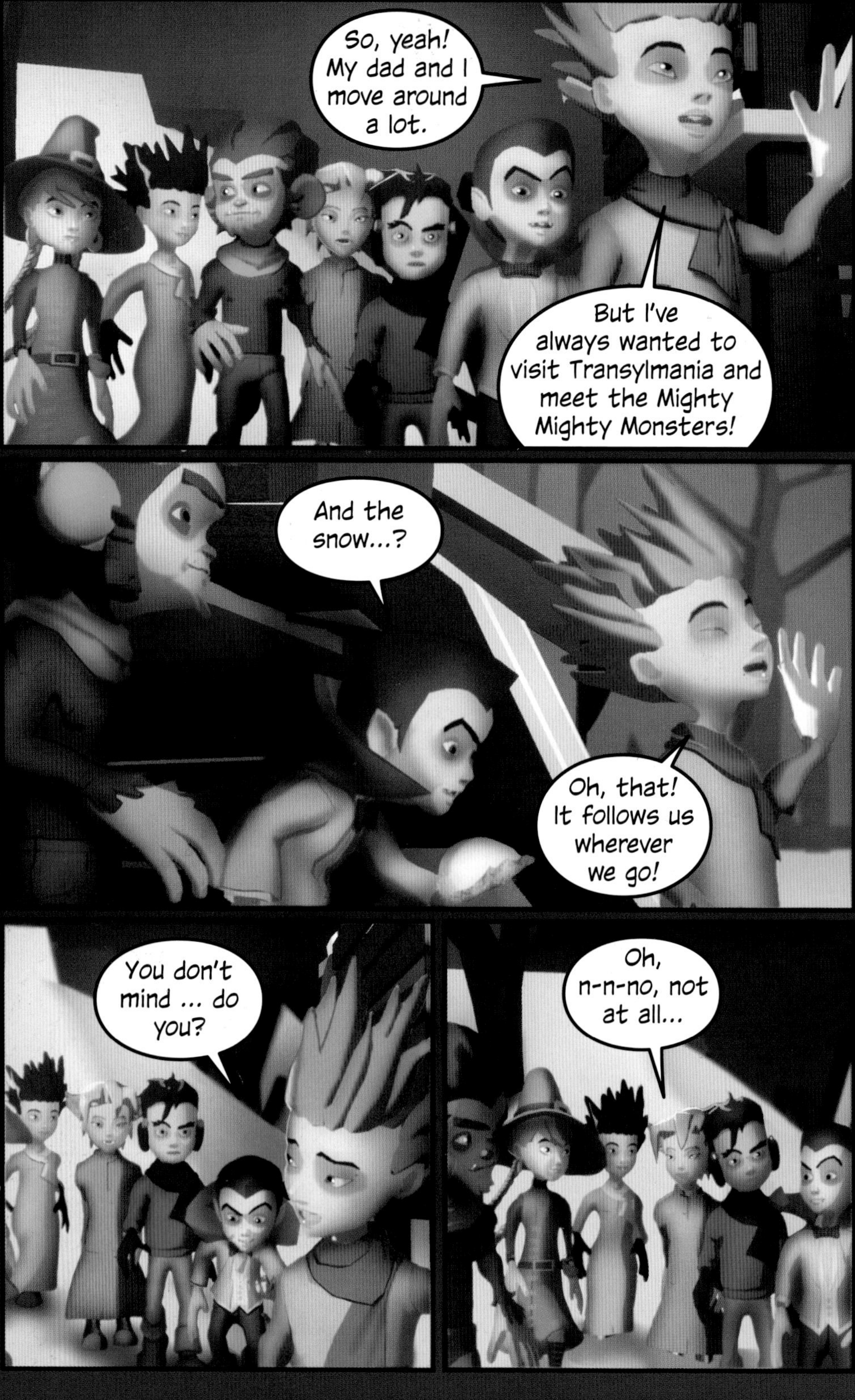
So, yeah! My dad and I move around a lot.
But I've always wanted to visit Transylmania and meet the Mighty Mighty Monsters!
And the snow...?
Oh, that! It follows us wherever we go!
You don't mind ... do you?
Oh, n-n-no, not at all...

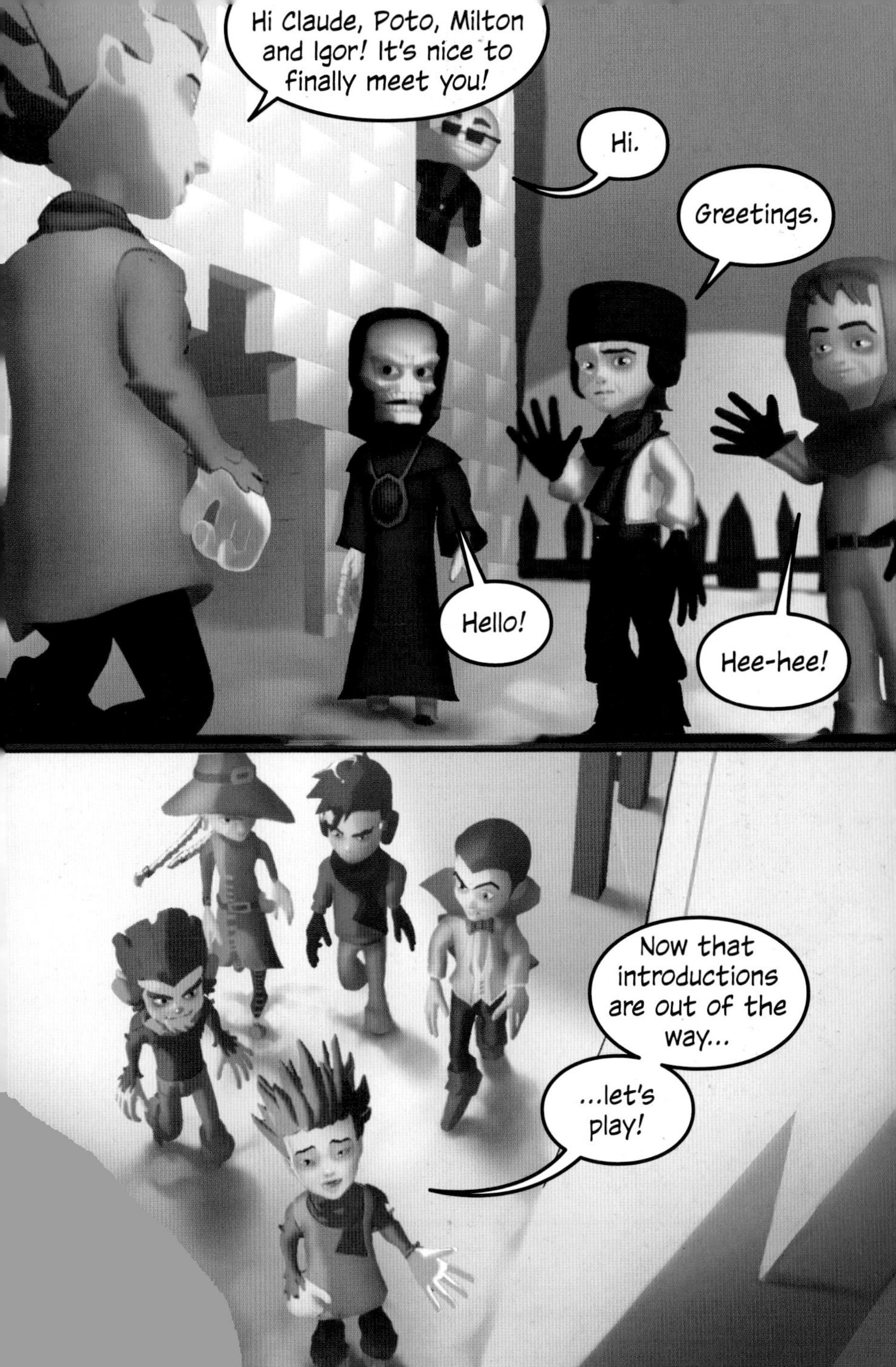
Hi Claude, Poto, Milton and Igor! It's nice to finally meet you!
Hi.
Greetings.
Hello!
Hee-hee!
Now that introductions are out of the way...
...let's play!
And play they did.

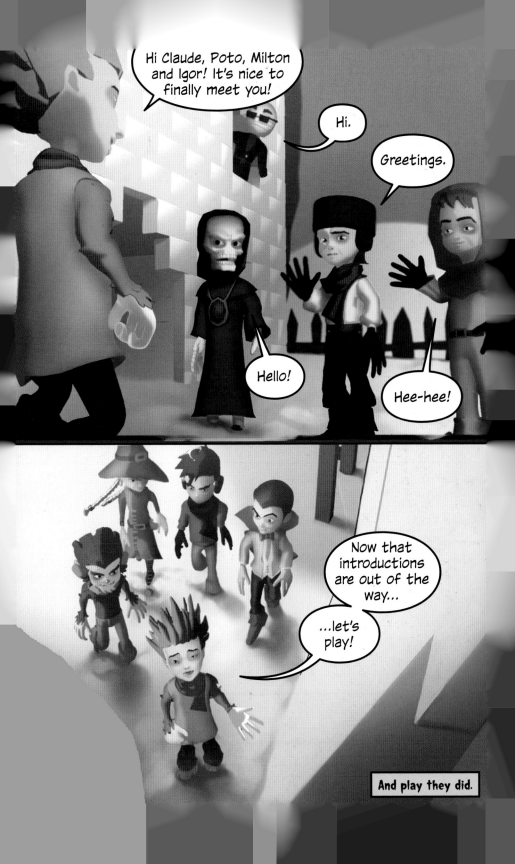

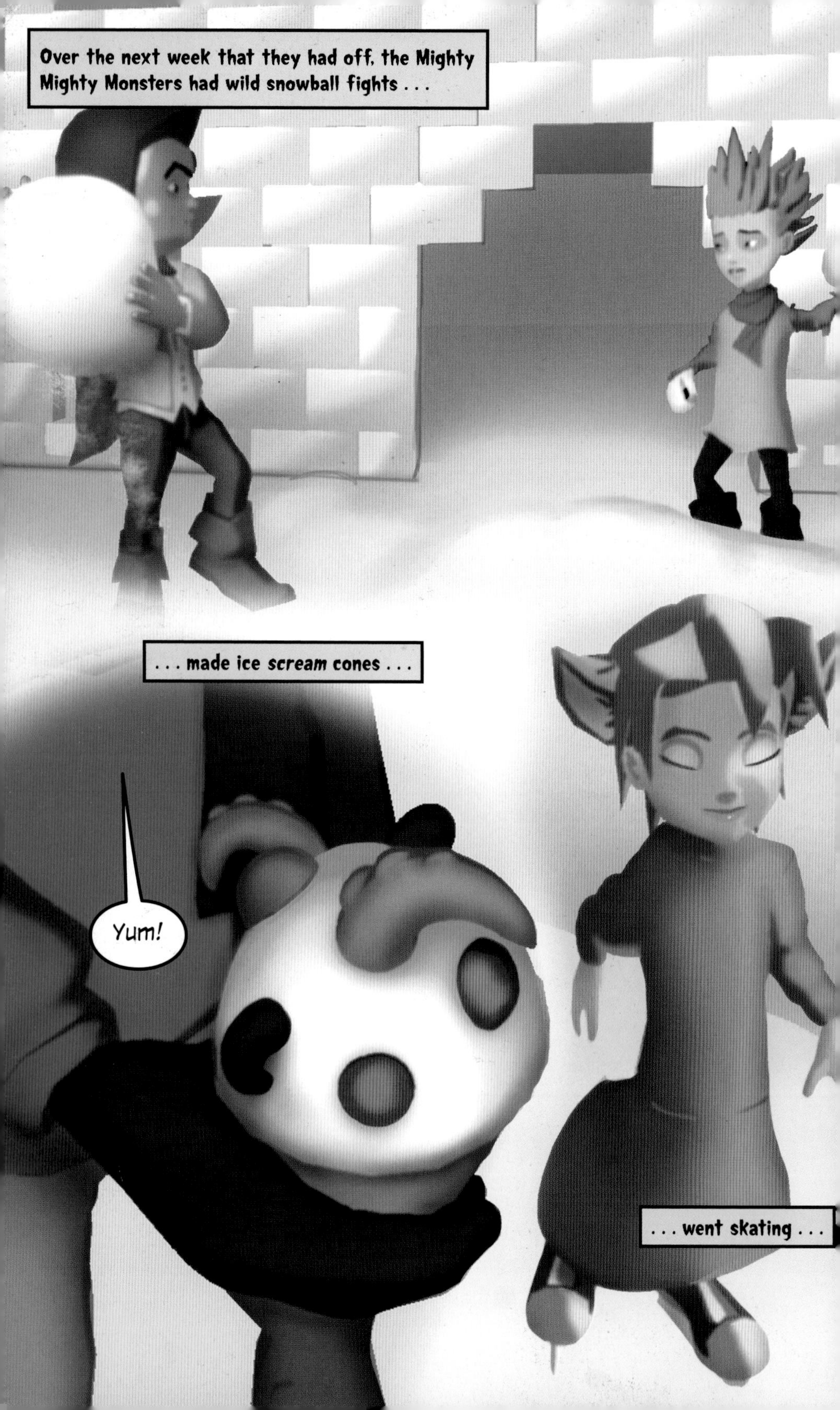
Over the next week that they had off, the Mighty Mighty Monsters had wild snowball fights . . .
. . . made ice *scream* cones . . .
Yum!
. . . went skating . . .

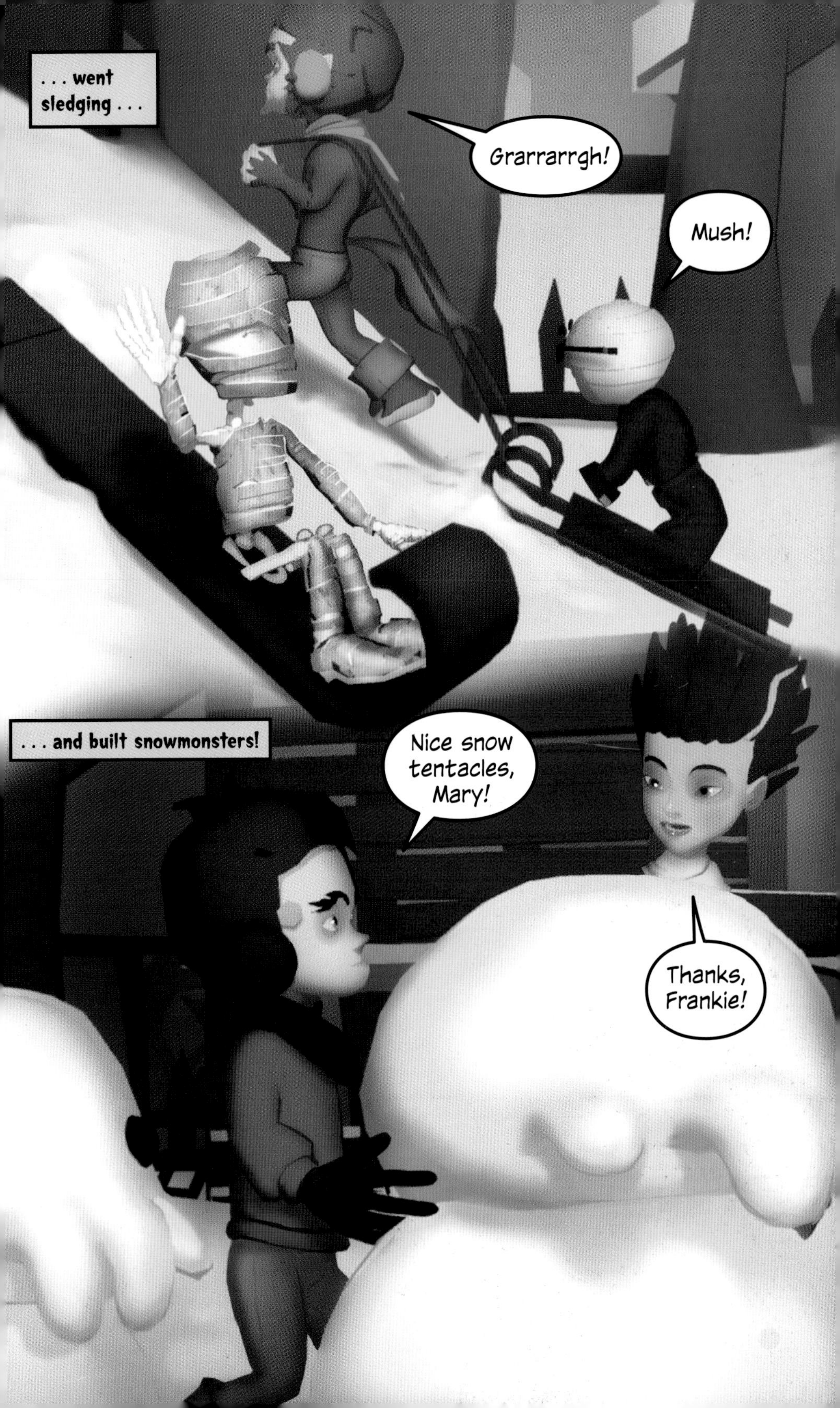
. . . went sledging . . .
Grarrarrgh!
Mush!
. . . and built snowmonsters!
Nice snow tentacles, Mary!
Thanks, Frankie!

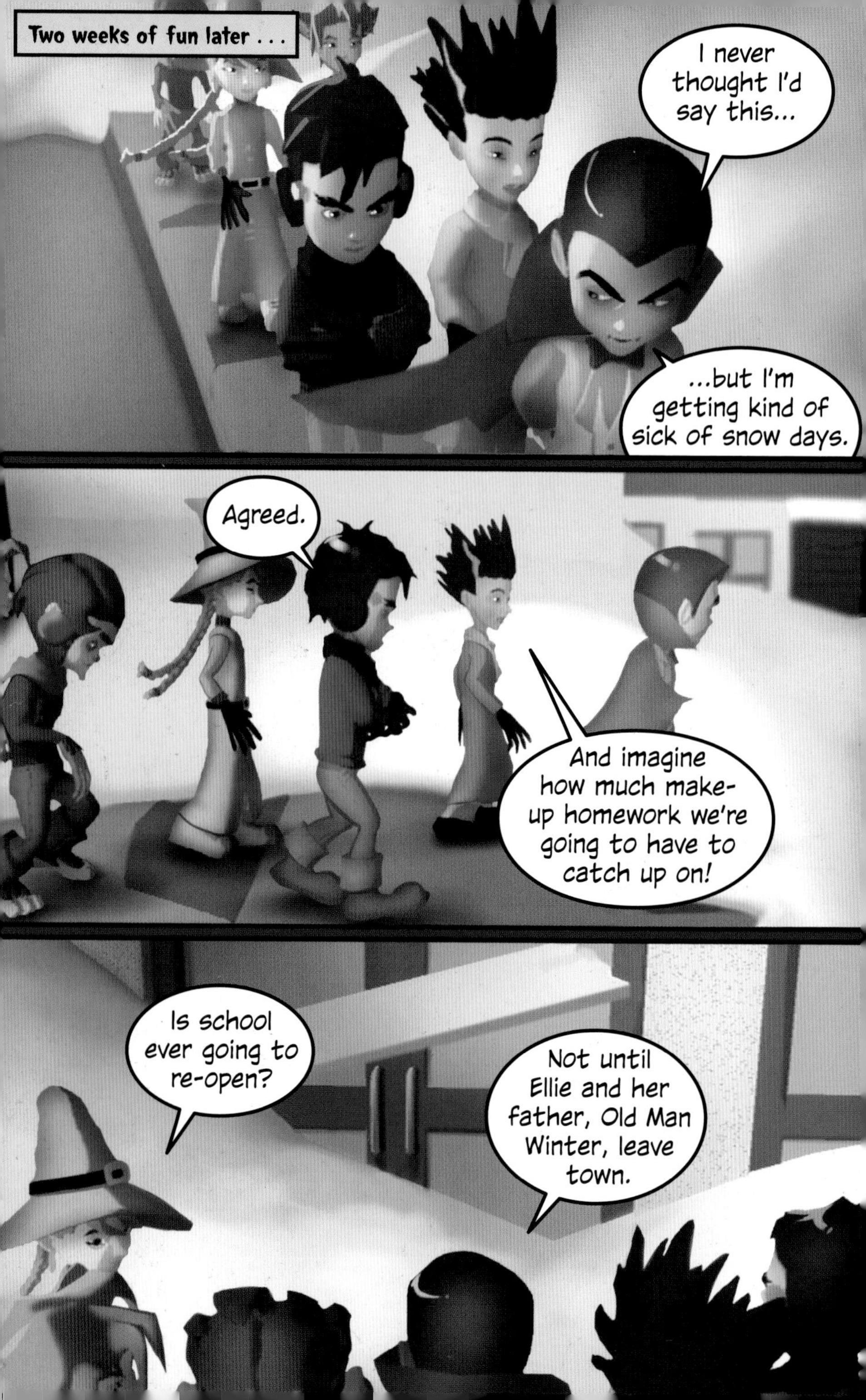
Two weeks of fun later . . .
I never thought I'd say this...
...but I'm getting kind of sick of snow days.
Agreed.
And imagine how much make-up homework we're going to have to catch up on!
Is school ever going to re-open?
Not until Ellie and her father, Old Man Winter, leave town.

29

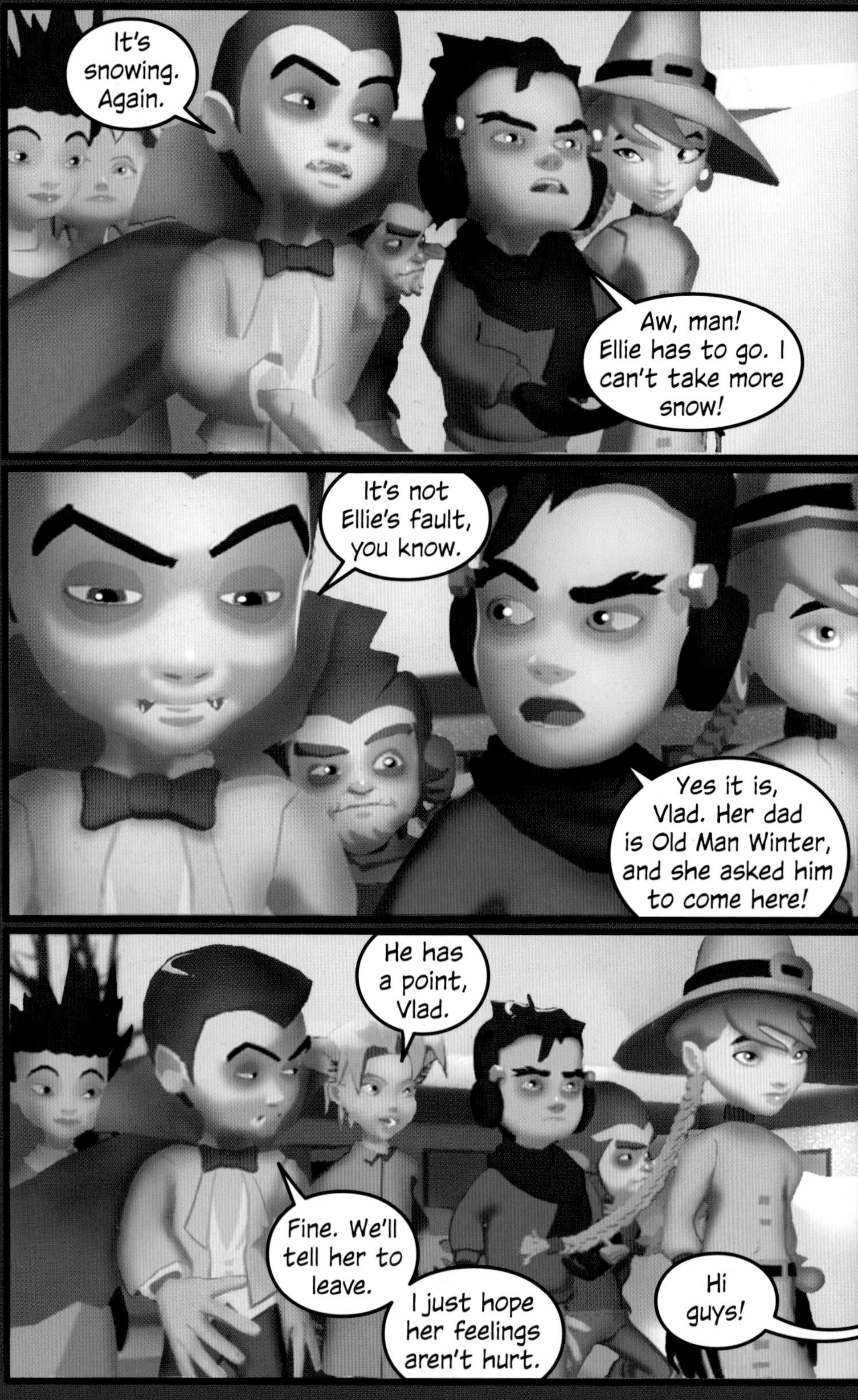
It's snowing. Again.
Aw, man! Ellie has to go. I can't take more snow!
It's not Ellie's fault, you know.
Yes it is, Vlad. Her dad is Old Man Winter, and she asked him to come here!
He has a point, Vlad.
Fine. We'll tell her to leave.
I just hope her feelings aren't hurt.
Hi guys!

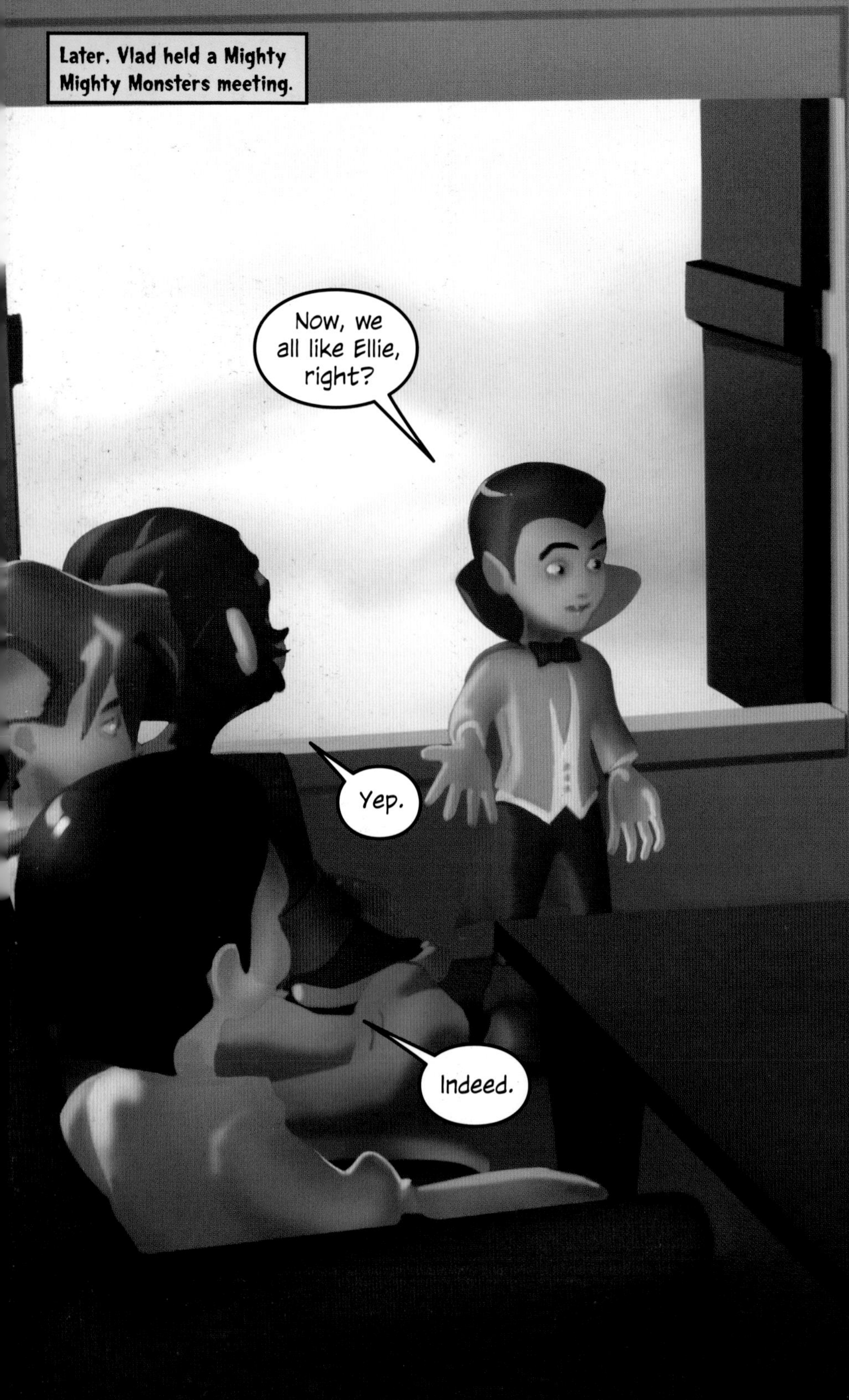
Later. Vlad held a Mighty Mighty Monsters meeting.
Now, we all like Ellie, right?
Yep.
Indeed.

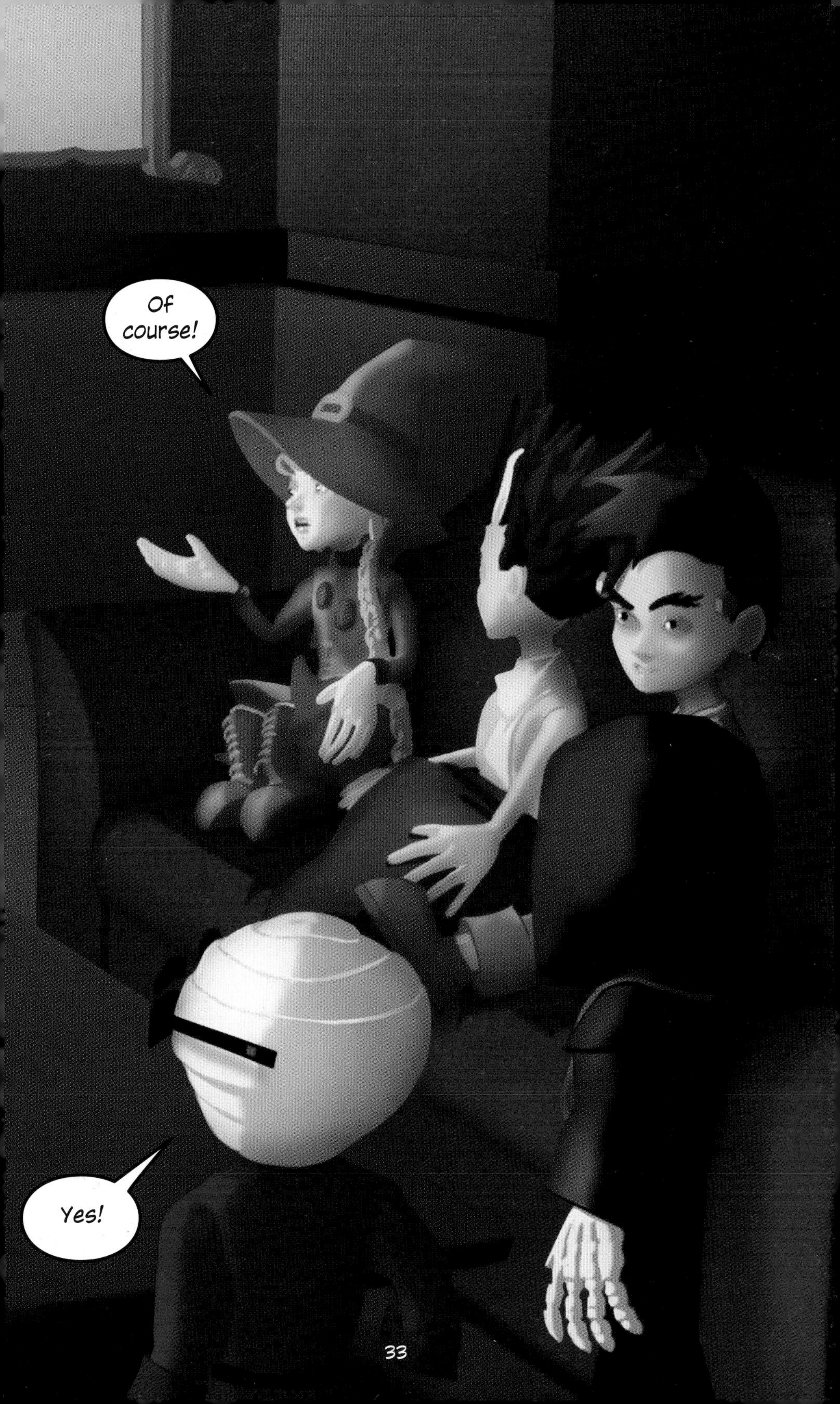
Of course!
Yes!

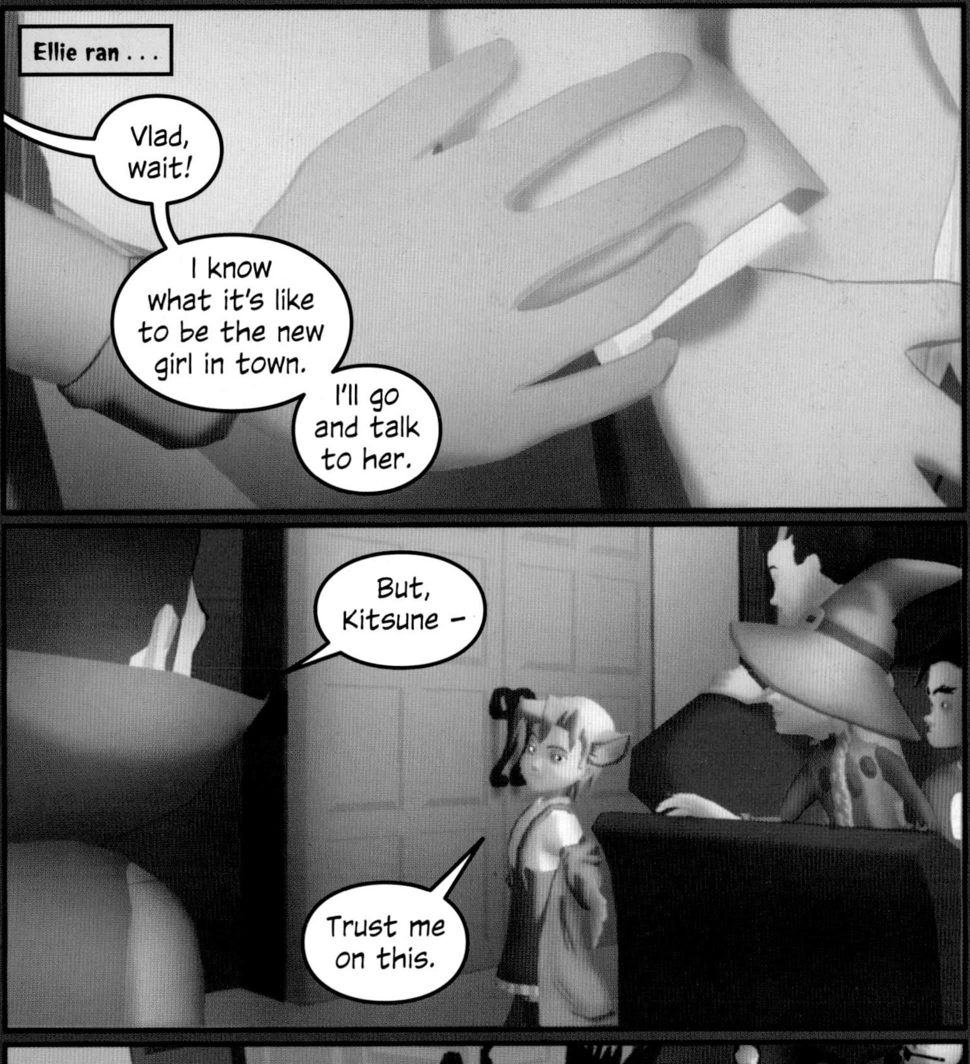
Ellie ran . . .
Vlad, wait!
I know what it's like to be the new girl in town.
I'll go and talk to her.
But, Kitsune –
Trust me on this.
I hope she's right.

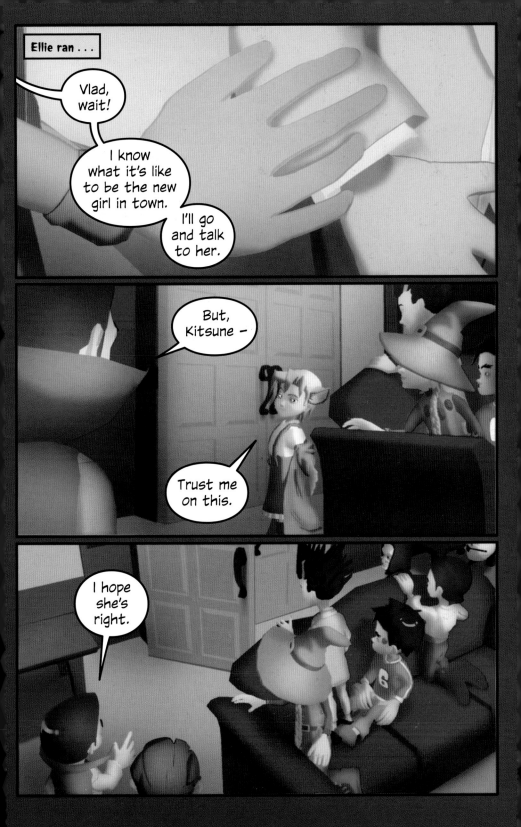

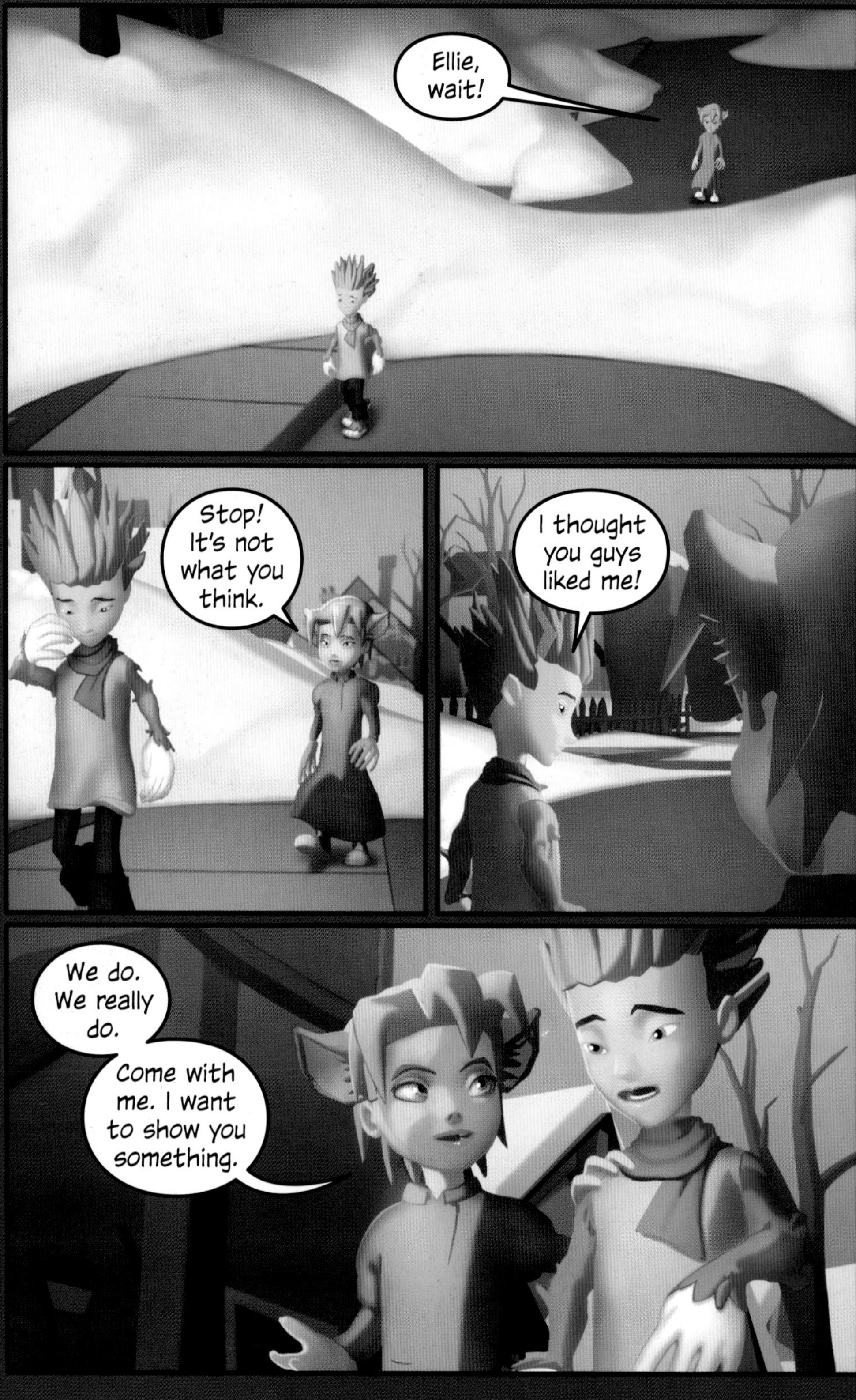
Ellie, wait!
Stop! It's not what you think.
I thought you guys liked me!
We do. We really do.
Come with me. I want to show you something.

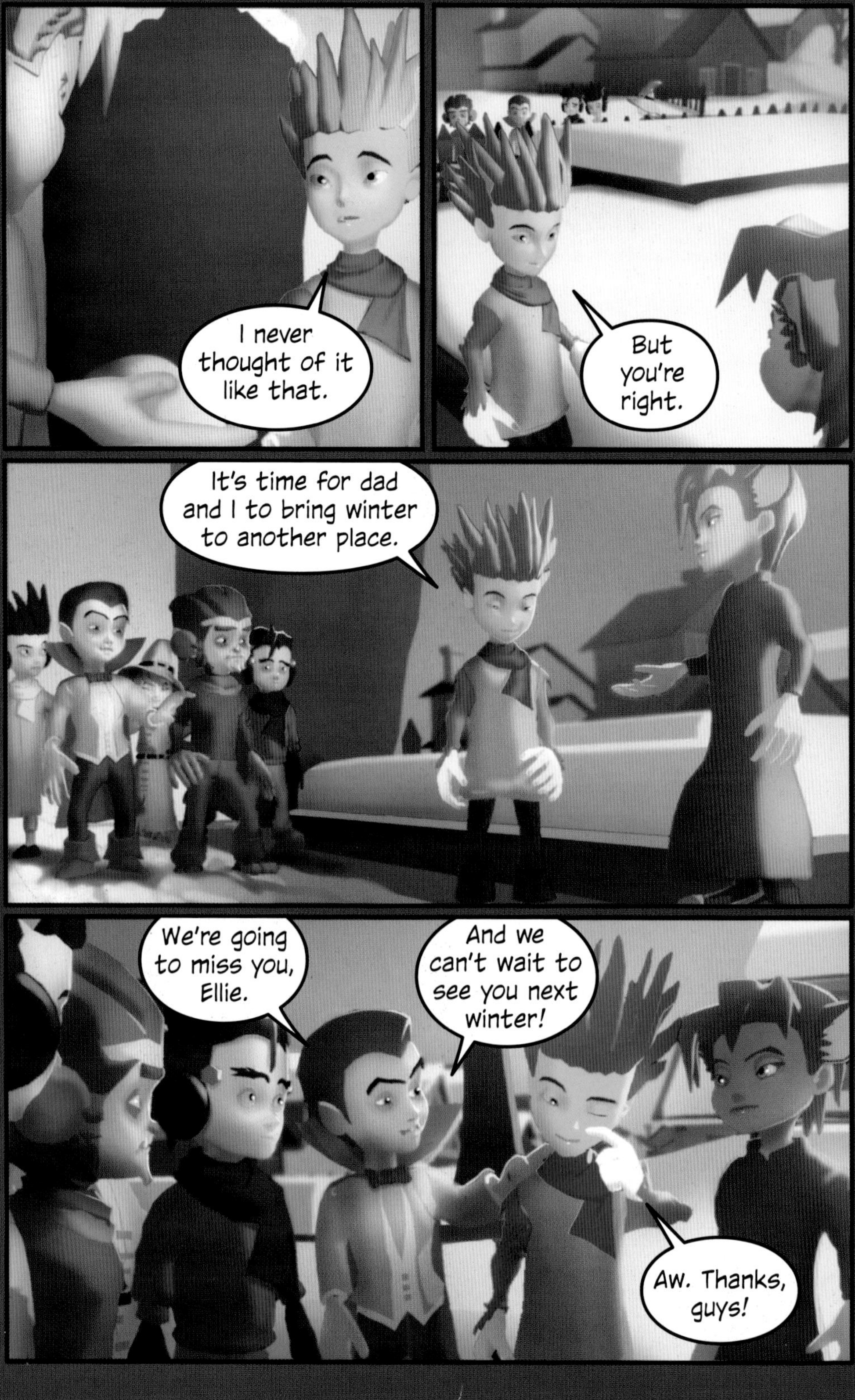
I never thought of it like that.
But you're right.
It's time for dad and I to bring winter to another place.
We're going to miss you, Ellie.
And we can't wait to see you next winter!
Aw. Thanks, guys!

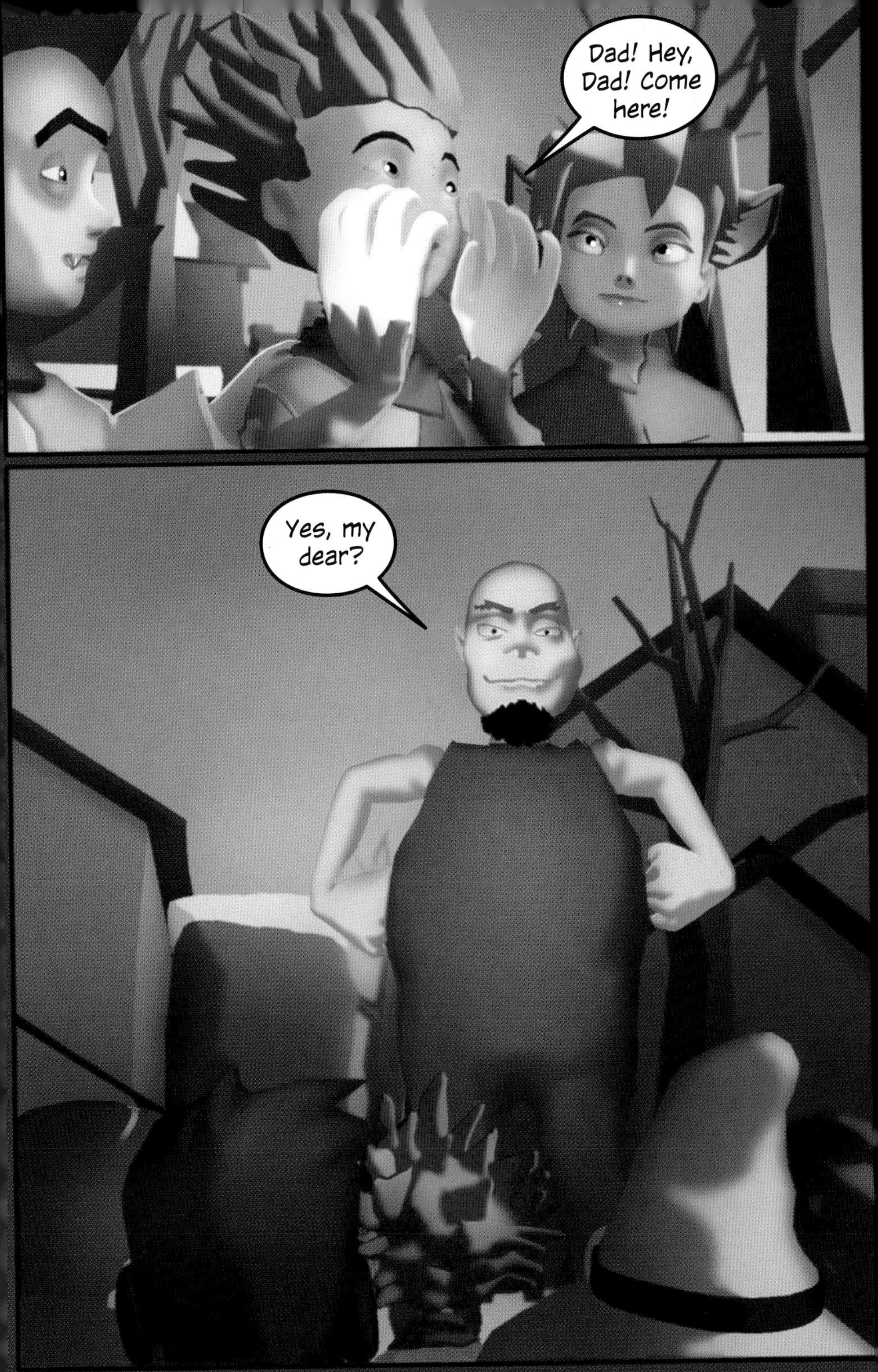
Dad! Hey, Dad! Come here!
Yes, my dear?

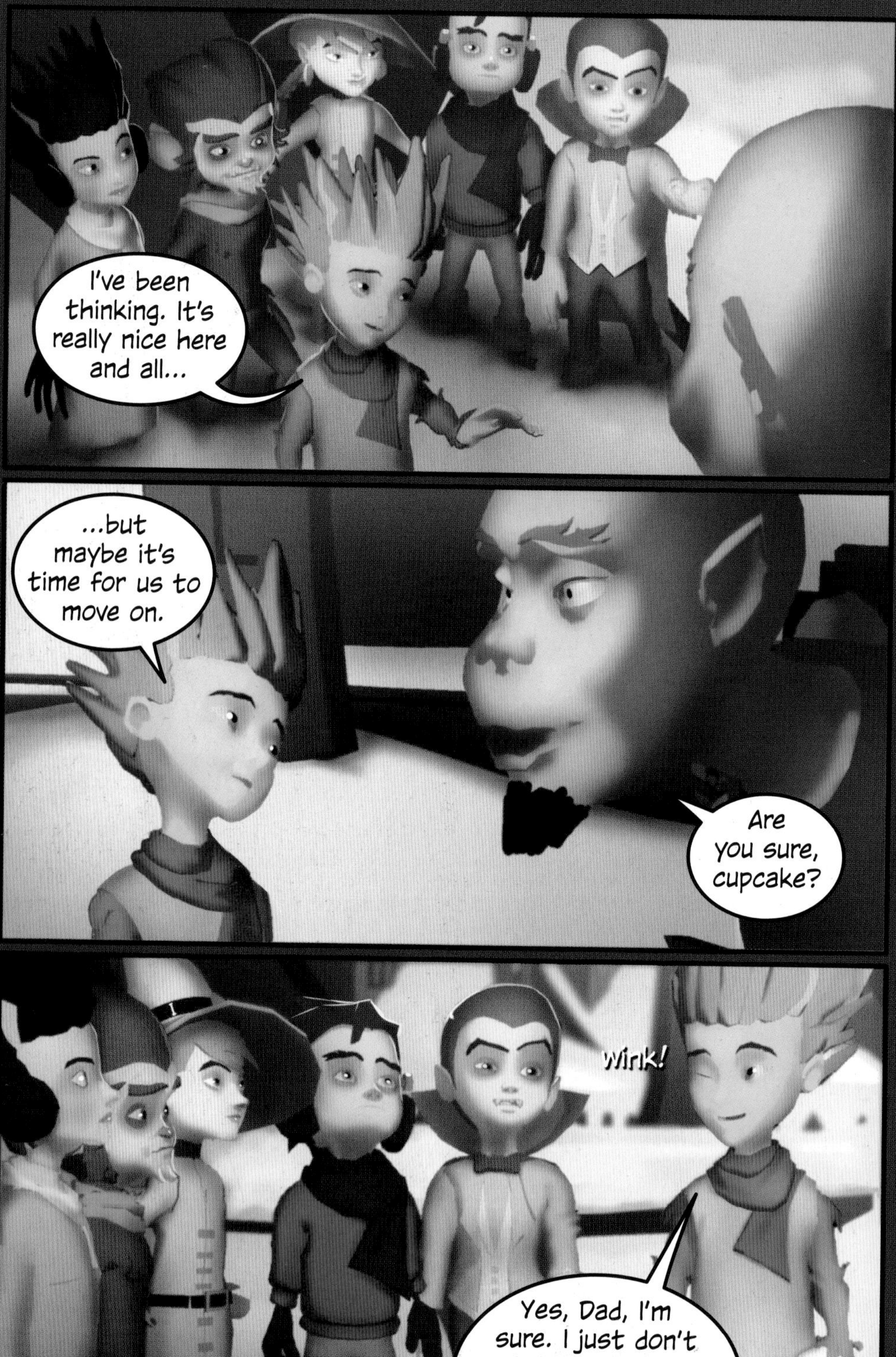
I've been thinking. It's really nice here and all...
...but maybe it's time for us to move on.
Are you sure, cupcake?
Wink!
Yes, Dad, I'm sure. I just don't want to get bored of this place, you know?

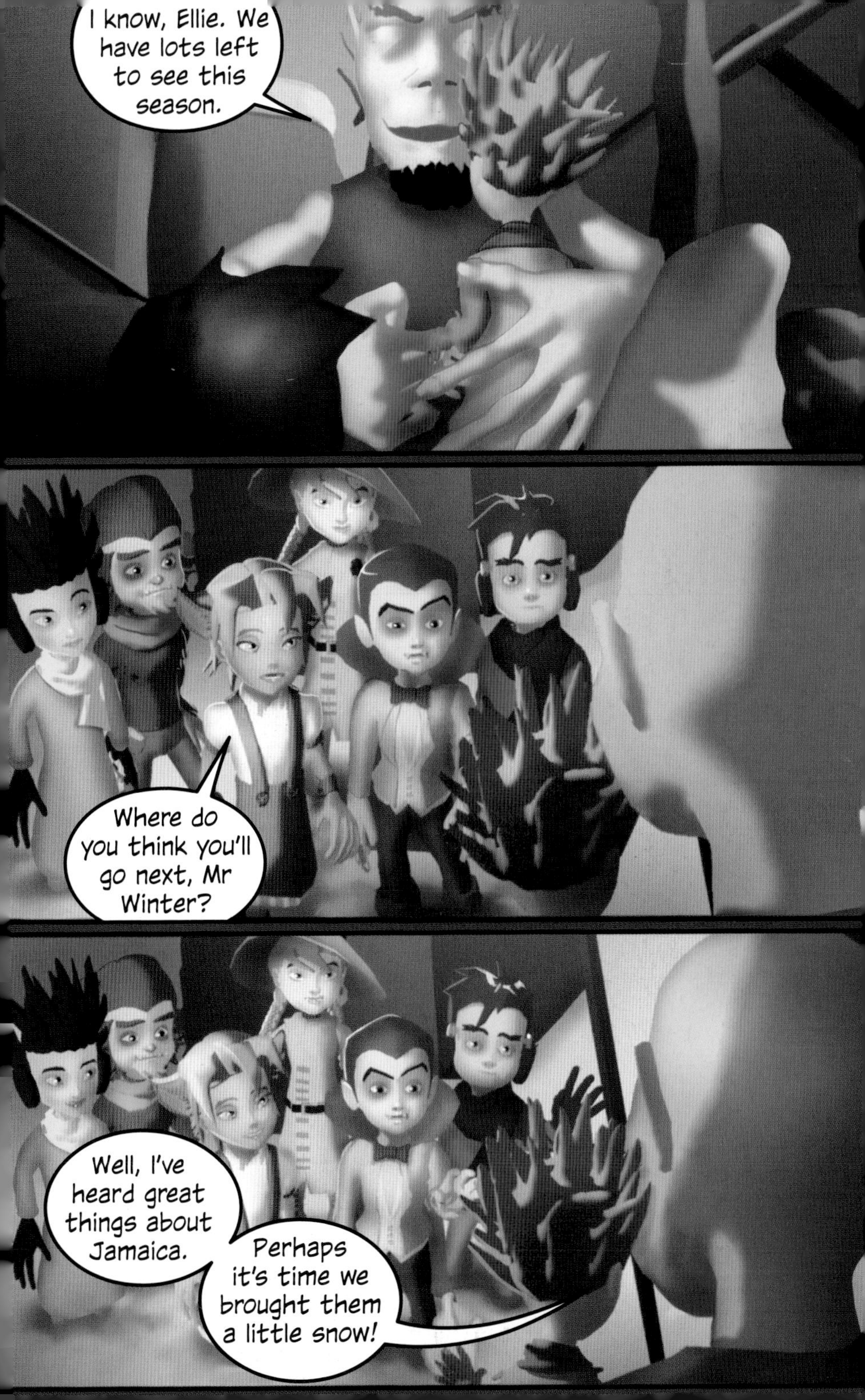

I know, Ellie. We have lots left to see this season.
Where do you think you'll go next, Mr Winter?
Well, I've heard great things about Jamaica.
Perhaps it's time we brought them a little snow!

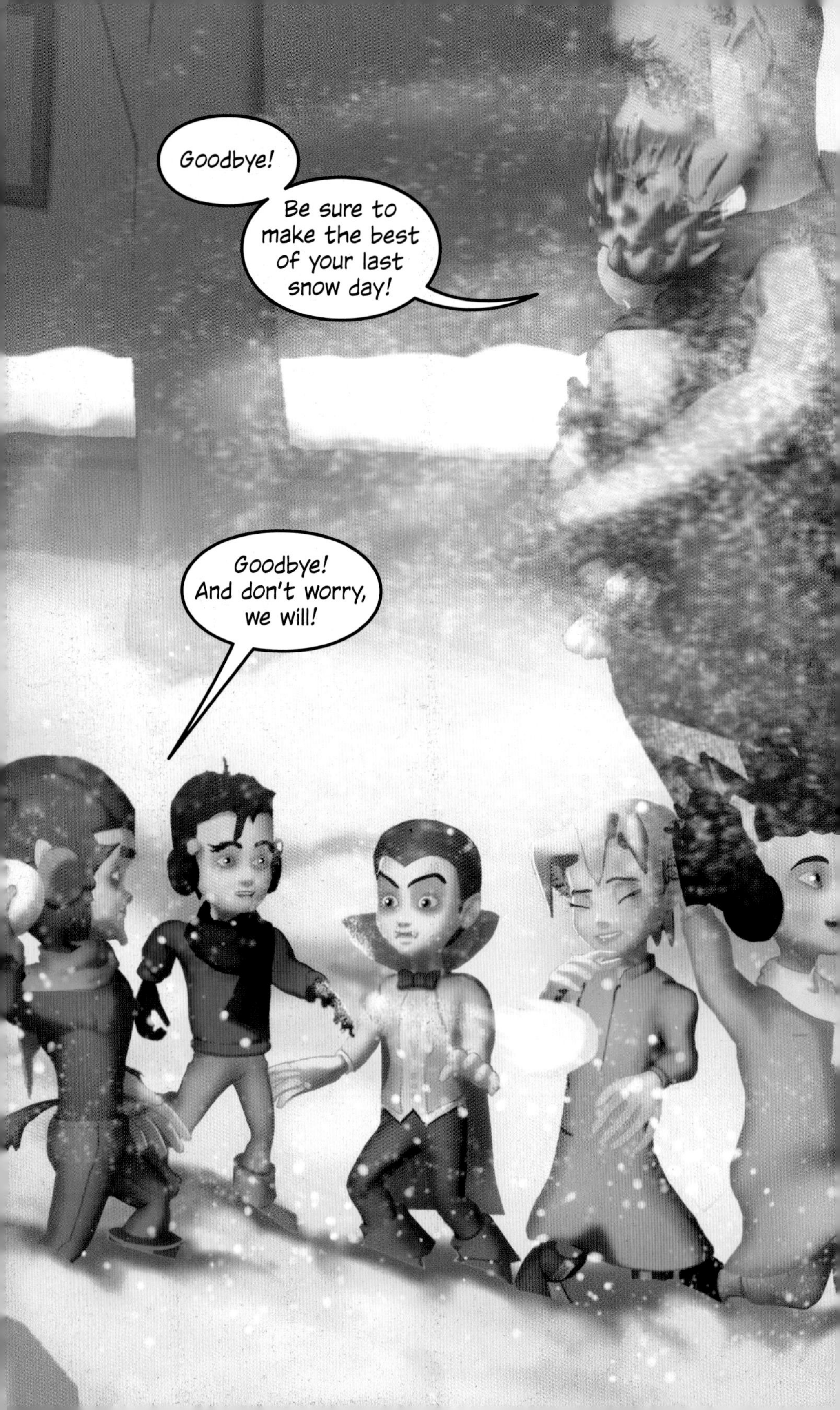

Goodbye!
Be sure to make the best of your last snow day!
Goodbye! And don't worry, we will!

ABOUT

SEAN O'REILLY

AND ARCANA STUDIO

As a lifelong comics fan, Sean O'Reilly dreamed of becoming a comic book creator. In 2004, he realized that dream by creating Arcana Studio. In one short year, O'Reilly took his studio from a one-person operation in his basement to an award-winning comic book publisher with more than 150 graphic novels produced for Harper Collins, Simon & Schuster, Random House, Scholastic and others.

Within a year, the company won many awards. O'Reilly also won the Top 40 Under 40 award from the city of Vancouver and authored *The Clockwork Girl* for Top Graphic Novel at Book Expo America in 2009. Currently, O'Reilly is one of the most prolific independent comic book writers in Canada. While showing no signs of slowing down in comics, he now writes screenplays and adapts his creations for the big screen.

GLOSSARY

appropriate (uh-PROH-pree-uht) – suitable for the situation, or right, as in appropriate clothing

blizzard (BLIZ-uhd) – a heavy snowstorm, often with strong winds

climate (KLYE-muht) – the usual weather in a certain place

curious (KYUR-ee-uhss) – eager to find something out, or interested in understanding how something works

honest (ON-ist) – an honest person is truthful and does not lie or steal or cheat

officially (uh-FISH-uhl-ee) – if something is official, it has been approved by someone in authority

relax (ri-LAKS) – to calm down, or become less tense and anxious

tentacles (TEN-tuh-kuhlz) – one of the long, flexible limbs of some animals like the octopus and squid

DISCUSSION QUESTIONS

1. Which Mighty Mighty Monster is your favourite? Why? Discuss your favourite monsters.

2. As long as Ellie is in Transylmania, there will never be another spring. If you could have only one season for the rest of your life, which one would you choose? Why?

3. Old Man Winter can travel anywhere in the world instantly. If you could teleport, where would you go? What places would you visit? Talk about travelling.

WRITING PROMPTS

1. Imagine another new monster has come to Transylmania. Who is he or she? Write about your new monster, and then draw a picture of him or her.

2. The Mighty Mighty Monsters get a snow day. What would you do if school was cancelled because of a blizzard? Write about your day off.

3. Even though they're friends, the gang has to tell Ellie to leave. Have you ever told someone you cared about something that wasn't easy to say? Write about it.

Mighty Mighty MONSTERS ADVENTURES

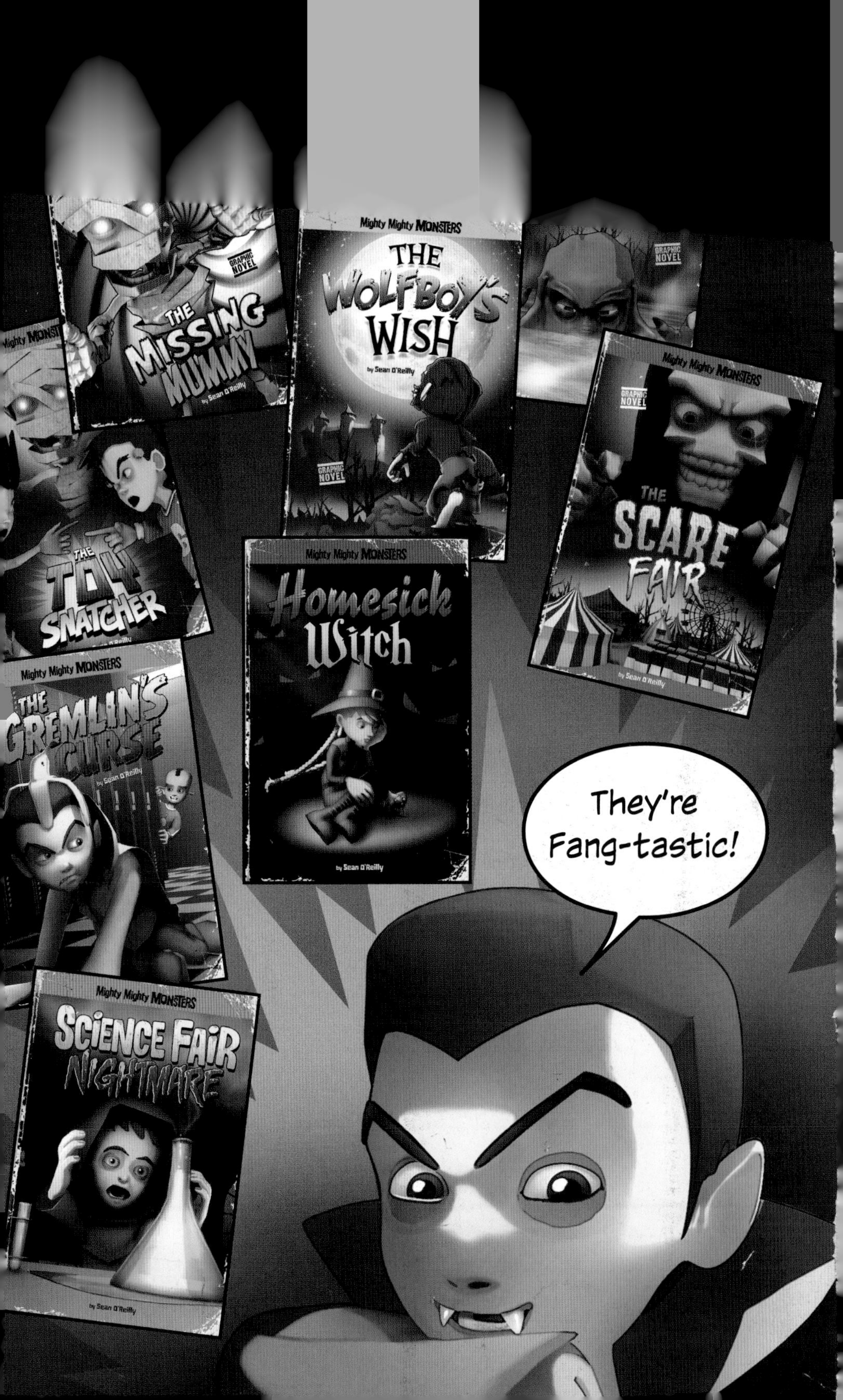

THE MISSING MUMMY
GRAPHIC NOVEL
by Sean O'Reilly
Mighty Mighty MONSTERS
THE WOLFBOY'S WISH
by Sean O'Reilly
GRAPHIC NOVEL
GRAPHIC NOVEL
Mighty Mighty MONSTERS
GRAPHIC NOVEL
THE SCARE FAIR
by Sean O'Reilly
THE TOY SNATCHER
Mighty Mighty MONSTERS
Homesick Witch
by Sean O'Reilly
Mighty Mighty MONSTERS
THE GREMLIN'S CURSE
by Sean O'Reilly
Mighty Mighty MONSTERS
SCIENCE FAIR NIGHTMARE
by Sean O'Reilly
They're Fang-tastic!

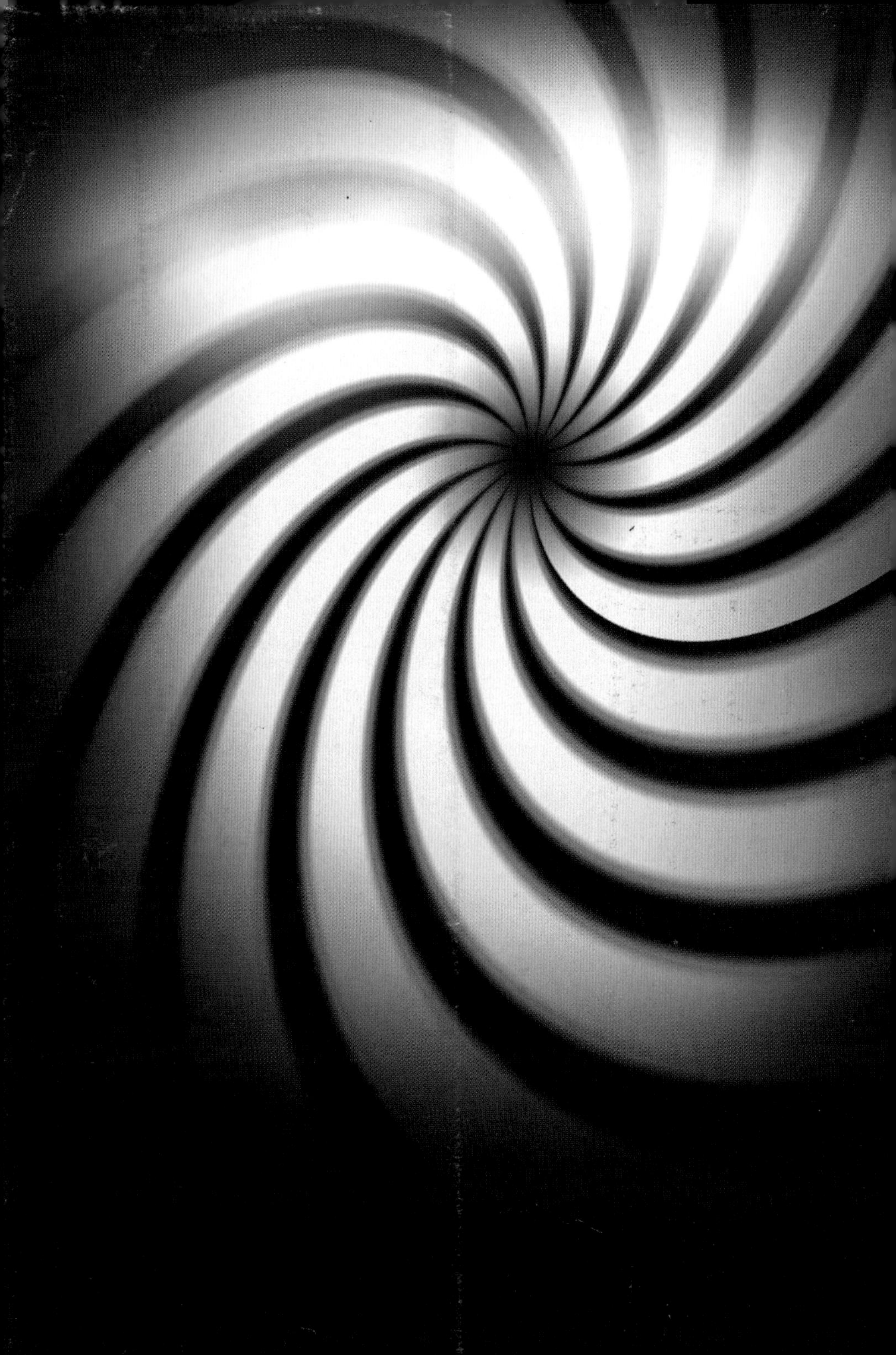

www.raintree.co.uk